ONCE UPON A DEAD MAN

Ben Stillman 7

PETER BRANDVOLD

WOLFPACK
PUBLISHING
— EST 2013 —

Once Upon A Dead Man
(Ben Stillman 7)

Kindle Edition
Copyright © 2019 (as revised) Peter Brandvold

Wolfpack Publishing
6032 Wheat Penny Ave
Las Vegas, NV 89122

wolfpackpublishing.com

Cover photography by Rick Evans Photography

eBook ISBN 978-1-64119-719-9
Paperback ISBN 978-1-64119-720-5

ONCE UPON A DEAD MAN

Chapter One

TWELVE PEACEABLE GYPSIES... MURDERED!

Silver star flashing on his cowhide vest, Marshal Charlie Boomhauer galloped his horse down the hill and into a narrow valley split by a shallow stream. At the bottom of the hill, he urged the skewbald gelding through the water, splashing and clattering over the rocks and flushing a pair of mallards to his right.

"He-yaw, horse, go!" Boomhauer coaxed the tired mount, spurring the animal harshly and slapping its right hip with a braided rawhide quirt as it bounded up the opposite ridge.

When he made the crest, Boomhauer halted the lathered horse beside the lone pine tree standing amidst rocks jutting up from the lush green grass. It was after the scraggly tree that the small town nestled in the valley below had been named.

Marshal Boomhauer stared down at Lone Pine now, giving himself and the skewbald a blow, getting his shaky nerves under control. He wondered what his next move should be--a move that he knew could very well mean not only the end of his job but the death of the little ranching village haphazardly scattered in the bowl of the rocky valley two hundred yards below him.

Twelve harmless Gypsies murdered and buried in a mass grave south of town, five miles deep in the Little Rocky Mountains...

Because of the grave he'd discovered less than a half hour ago, there was anger as well as fear in Charlie Boomhauer, and it was the anger that finally propelled him off the ridge and into town at a gallop. When he came to the main drag, Crawford Street, he slowed the horse to a canter, then pulled up at the tie rail before the Lone Pine State Bank.

Betty Jean Davison's Millinery and Dress-Making Shop sat across the street. The three ladies visiting out front, dressed in fashionable gowns and straw hats, watched with open curiosity as the town marshal—a short, gray-haired, bandy-legged gent in his late fifties—dismounted from his horse with an audible curse, his upturned eyebrows beetled with agitation. The ladies weren't accustomed to seeing old Charlie Boomhauer, the easy-going drover-turned-marshal, driven to such an obvious frazzle.

"Casey!" the old marshal yelled to one of the two boys bouncing a ball off the side of Bill Mason's smokehouse behind the bank. "Take my horse over to the livery and tell Dewey Seton I want a buckboard wagon hitched to two mules! You got that?"

The towheaded boy of ten, wearing dirty bib-front coveralls, had already come running, holding his leather-billed immigrant hat on his head. "Got it, Marshal. What's goin' on?"

"Just do as I say, boy," the marshal ordered. He flipped the boy a dime, then turned on his stovepipe boots and grunted up the three steps to the bank.

When he pushed through the door, he did not take

time to greet either of the two tellers in their cages. Instead, he turned to his left, pushed through the gate in the low wood fence, walked past the vice president and loan clerk without so much as a nod, and without knocking, pushed through the door at the back of the room.

Stepping into the president's office, he gave the door a careless heave, slamming it. He pinned his stern, squinting gaze to the stout gentleman seated behind a broad, hide-covered desk flanked by an oversized safe, and asked, "Did you do it, Mr. Drake? Did you do what I think ye done?"

Wilfred B. Drake, owner and president of the Lone Pine State Bank, scowled across the green-bound ledger open before him, pen in one hand, Cuban cigar in the other. Drake was a stout man with close-cropped, steel-gray hair receding at the temples. He wore a walrus mustache, round spectacles, and a square-cut, black suit with a clay worsted vest and foulard tie. Before him stood a green-bowled lamp, a hand-carved cigar box with his gold initials set in the lid, and a silver tray bearing a heavy port decanter and four crystal tumblers.

Drake's jowls quivered and his face mottled as he jerked a glance behind him, at the photograph of Rutherford B. Hayes, which had been jarred crooked by the slamming door. The picture was still swinging as Drake turned back to the marshal.

"Charlie—what in the hell is the meaning of this?"

"Did ye? Did ye do what I think ye done, Mr. Drake?"

"What on earth are you talking about?" Drake asked, staring at the marshal from behind his glinting spectacles, befuddled and annoyed. Gesturing to the upholstered parlor chair before his desk, he said, "Settle down, now, Marshal. Take a seat."

Boomhauer shook his head. "I don't want no seat. I

wanna know if ye did it. I wanna know if ye killed them Gypsies."

The banker scowled as though trying to communicate with a deaf-mute. "What Gypsies?"

"Them that been campin' outside town, in the mountains."

"They're dead? *All* of them?"

"As far as I can tell. I didn't see 'em, but I saw the grave, and I didn't see none living. Got word there'd been trouble that way, so I rode out there by that spring, where those cottonwoods grow, an' seen a couple of Crawford's late heifers standin' around lookin' owly as all get-out."

"You sure you didn't just come upon an old buffalo camp, Charlie?"

"There weren't never no buffalo camp out there. I'd know. I been in these parts a good twenty-five years. I tell you what I do know, Mr. Drake. I know where those Gypsies were camped, and I know the camp ain't there anymore. The grass is all matted where they pitched their tents, and their fire rings are still here, but their tents an' wagons are gone. And you know what else? There's a suspicious-looking mound, covered with rocks, at the bottom of the ravine south of the camp."

Drake watched Boomhauer steadily, both hands on his desk, puffing his stogie. He blinked several times, pushed his chair out, and stood with a sigh. Removing the cigar from his mouth with his right hand, he strode across the carpet and looked out the window, at Lone Pine's typically sluggish afternoon traffic—mostly farm and ranch wagons, boys and girls released from school, occasional housewives heading to the mercantile for odds and ends they'd forgotten to pick up that morning.

Drake replaced the cigar in his mouth and entwined

his hands behind his back. "Who told you there was trouble out mere?" he asked the marshal with a wistful air.

"Can't tell you that, Mr. Drake."

Boomhauer's voice was still hard, but there was a hint of apology in it as well. After all, Wilfred Drake had pulled this town up by its bootstraps. Not only that, he'd helped Boomhauer get appointed as marshal. If not for Drake, the town would still be little more than a watering hole for drovers, and a stage relay station. Boomhauer himself would still be chasing steers on that little ten-cow operation he'd attempted out by Aspen Creek—fighting spring rains, winter snows, and his bad left hip.

Yes, Wilfred Drake had shed a lot of sweat building this town. He'd put up a lot of capital, and Charlie Boomhauer owed him. But that didn't mean the banker should get away with the murder of a dozen innocent Gypsies, half of them women and children!

"What makes you think I had anything to do with it?" the banker asked dully, still staring out at the street.

The marshal watched the heavyset man, letting several seconds pass. His gut ached from the gravity of the problem—twelve people doubtless dead, a pillar of the community no doubt responsible. Bringing Drake down might cause a run on the bank and destroy the town.

His anger waning, his voice betrayed his sadness and frustration. "You know why, Mr. Drake."

Drake wheeled to him, his face flushing again. He started to say something, cut it off, and started on a different thread, beginning with a phony laugh. "I couldn't have murdered a dozen Gypsies. Why..."

"You hired it done."

"Yeah? Who would I hire to do such a thing?"

"I don't know," Boomhauer said. "And I doubt I can

find out—not with you pullin' the town's strings like you do. But I know who can."

The banker studied him, as befuddled as before. "Who...? What...?" Lifting his hands, palms out, he said, "Whoa, now... wait just a minute, Charlie. I don't know what you got up your sleeve, but you better take that seat I offered and cool off a bit. Pour yourself a brandy. You don't want to go off half-way. I mean, you don't even have proof a crime was committed. For all you know, those Gypsies headed back to Canada."

"I hope they did, Mr. Drake," Boomhauer said sincerely. "And that's just what I aim to find out." With that, Boomhauer tugged his hat lower on his head and turned to the door. When he reached it, he stopped and turned half around. "I hope I'm wrong, Mr. Drake. I really hope I'm wrong. But I got a chill deep in that bad hip o' mine that tells me I'm not."

"Charlie, get back here and have a seat! We have to talk about this."

"Mr. Drake," Boomhauer said, turning his sullen eyes on the banker. "I've done just about everything you've ever asked me to do. But there's one thing I just can't do, and that's turn my back on murder. If I do that, I might just as well pack it in right now, spend the rest of my life in a rockin' chair."

Boomhauer opened the door and went out.

"Charlie, damnit, get back here!" Drake bellowed behind him.

The sullen but determined Boomhauer walked out of the bank, turned right, and headed for the livery barn. His spurs chinged on the boardwalk, his holstered six-gun flapped on his thigh, and his stomach felt as though he'd swallowed a railroad spike.

Back inside the bank, Wilfred Drake stuck his red face

through his office door and bellowed to the loan officer, "Eddie, get Nick Corey in here—pronto!"

"I'm here, I'm here, Mr. Drake," said a man slouched in a Windsor chair to the left of Drake's door, his long legs extended, his worn boots crossed at the ankles. His battered brown Stetson sat on his right knee. "I heard about the marshal stormin' into town like a donkey with its tail on fire, an' I figgered one, or the other of you'd want me." A youthful, sandy-haired man wearing a deputy marshal's star on his deer-hide vest, Nick Corey *smiled* with his usual mocking irony.

Drake scowled at him. How was it the deputy always seemed to know when Drake was going to need him— before Drake did himself? "Shut up and get in here, Nick!"

———

"*HE-YAA! HE-YAA, MULES, HE-YAAAAA!*" Charlie Boomhauer yelled as he slapped the reins against the backs of the two geldings hitched to the buckboard.

He'd been on the twisting, turning wagon road for nearly a half hour now, driving the team so hard he was afraid the rattling buckboard carrying two shovels, a pick, several lanterns, a canteen, a sack of jerky, and two tarpaulins was going to come apart at the seams and deposit him and his load on the trail. But he wanted to make it to the gravesite before dark, to at least get a start on his grisly task before the sun went down.

Around him, the rounded, rocky peaks of the Little Rocky Mountains humped, blocking out the horizon. The pine-covered slopes were dotted with wildflowers, and the western ridges were turning rose-pink as the sun angled low, luring shadows from swales and ravines, and bringing the mule deer down from their rocky haunts to nibble the breeze-ruffled bluestem and buffalo grass in the meadows.

It was a serene time of the day, with the meadowlarks cooing and the sunlight softening, the air perfumed with mown grass and chokecherry blossoms. But not even the lovely sprays of bluebonnets could abate the winter storm raging in Charlie Boomhauer's mind. Today, with his grisly discovery, his life had changed, and nothing around here would ever be the same again. He was descending a rocky saddle through which the road cut when he heard a muffled yell behind him. Turning in the wagon box, he squinted northward and saw a horse and rider galloping toward him—the man's face a sun-splashed oval beneath the brim of his brown Stetson.

Curious, Boomhauer slowed the mules to a walk and watched the horseman approach.

"Nick, what in the hell are you doin' here?" Boomhauer groused as the deputy approached on his blowing, blaze-faced dun. "You should be back in town, keepin' an eye on things."

"I figured you needed me out here, Marshal," Corey said, riding beside the wagon, slouched in his saddle, smiling his affable smile. "When I heard from Dewey Seton that you left town with a wagon and shovels, I thought I better tag along, see if you needed some help."

"*If* I needed help, I would've sent Casey for you," Boomhauer barked, none too pleased with the deputy's appearance.

There was no denying that Nick Corey was an effective deputy. Easily young enough to be Boomhauer's son, Corey was better at bracing criminals and keeping the saloons civil than Boomhauer himself. But Boomhauer, while never able to pinpoint why, had never really trusted the young man. There was just something about the always-grinning Corey that seemed at once phony and sneering, as though he had the upper hand on you and was waiting for the right opportunity to bring it down.

He would not have been the marshal's first choice for a deputy, but eighteen months ago, when Boomhauer's previous deputy quit and left the country, Wilfred Drake had pressured Boomhauer into hiring Corey, who'd once punched cows for the biggest spread in the county, Max Crawford's Snaketrack.

Now the supercilious deputy shrugged his broad shoulders, grinning, and said, "You know, I figured you'd say that, Marshal. Yessiree, there's no more capable man in the land than you. But, well, I just figured I'd lend you a' hand, that's all. What can it hurt? The town's been quiet enough, an' it's a weeknight, so none of the cowpokes'll be in...."

Boomhauer only grumbled. What could he say? Corey had a point. He always had a point...

After they'd ridden for a while, Boomhauer walking and trotting his team in turns, Corey said, "You haven't told me where we're headin' yet, Marshal."

"You'll see soon enough," Boomhauer crisply replied. He didn't trust the big, smiling deputy with the key to his own desk—how could he trust him with this? He'd know soon enough.

"Marshal," Corey spoke when they'd ridden several more minutes, "what do you say you and me turn around now, and head on home?

Charlie Boomhauer jerked a suspicious look at the deputy riding slouched in his saddle, head canted to one side as he peered straight ahead. "Why's that, Nick?"

Corey shrugged.

"You talk to Drake, did ye?"

Corey pursed his lips and gave his head a lazy shake. "Nope. I never talked to no one. I didn't have to. I can tell just by lookin' at you and them shovels and whatnot in that wagon... we best turn around an' go home."

"You go ahead, Nick," Boomhauer said, flicking his reins across the mules' backs. "Turn around and go on home. I didn't call you out here in the first place."

"Nah," Corey said. "I reckon I'll tag along... give ye a hand..."

Boomhauer studied the deputy across his shoulder, feeling even more leery of the man than usual. He adjusted the six-gun on his hip and returned his attention to the road, which forked about fifty yards ahead. Boomhauer took the right fork and soon found himself and the deputy passing a run-out spring in a hollow and continuing around a flat-topped butte to a stream. They followed the stream about a hundred yards south, through pines and scattered aspens, and then the marshal brought the wagon to a halt on the lip of a steep-walled ravine through which the stream trickled.

The valley was in full shade now, as the sun had slipped behind the western ridge. The sky still offered some light, however. The air was noticeably cooler.

"Why... by the way the grass is all matted hereabouts, I'd swear people have camped here," Corey said, dramatically, almost mockingly. He sat on his tail-swishing horse and gazed around as Boomhauer set the brake and climbed down from the buckboard.

"That's right," the marshal said with a grunt.

He lifted a shovel from the wagon bed and walked to the edge of the ravine and looked down. The cutbank had been broken off and caved into the ravine. The silty soil formed a mound below the new rim, and the mound had been covered with rocks.

"I believe they're down here," Boomhauer said gravely.

"If that's so," Corey said with an air of frustration, "where's their wagons?"

"I'll look for them later after we've dug up the bodies."

The deputy studied the marshal as Boomhauer, clutching his shovel, sat down on the bank and eased himself over the edge. The old man was driven down the steep incline by gravity, tripping and nearly falling in the loose soil. When he made the bottom and got himself stopped, he caught his breath, studied the rock-covered mound for a while, and shook his head.

He kicked away several rocks and lowered the spade, stabbing it into the dirt with his boot.

Corey scowled and shook his head. With a sigh, he dismounted from his horse, tied the animal to the rear of the wagon, and lifted the second shovel from the box. Shaking his head again, he started walking toward Boomhauer, who was digging steadily, puffing and sweating with the effort.

The mules hung their heads in the traces and watched the two men with dull-eyed curiosity.

Who could know what they were wondering as they watched the old marshal and the young deputy digging in the ravine below as the sun sank even farther behind the western ridge, casting the valley in even denser shadow?

Who could know what they thought when they saw the young man stop digging suddenly, turn to the old man who'd let his guard down, lift his spade like a club, and bring it down hard against the back of the old man's skull?

Boomhauer gave a grunt His knees buckled as, head down, he took two feeble steps forward, then dropped on the mound with a groan.

The mules twitched their ears and rippled their sides, watching the younger man move to the marshal. Corey drew his heavy, long-barreled Colt, aimed at the prone, groaning figure of Charlie Boomhauer, and pulled the trigger.

The mules jumped with the flat report, sidestepping.

They watched Corey lift the old man over his shoulder, carry him up the ravine, drop him inside the wagon, and cover his inert body with a tarp.

That done, Corey returned to the ravine for the shovels and replaced the rocks Boomhauer had moved. When he'd dropped the shovels in the wagon box, he climbed aboard, took up the reins, clucked to the mules, and turned them back the way they'd come, his horse following along behind the wagon.

Corey took his time heading back to town. But when he was two miles away, he put the mules into a breakneck gallop, kicking up dust and making a thunderous clatter. He stormed through the dark, star-capped village of Lone Pine, shouting at the mules, skidding around corners, and setting the dogs to wailing.

When he pulled up before a small, blue-frame house nestled in flowering lilacs, he hurriedly set the brake and jumped to the ground.

"Oh, Mrs. Boomhauer!" he yelled at the house in which a single lamp shone. "Come quick! Something just *awful's* happened!"

Chapter Two

BEN STILLMAN, SHERIFF OF HILL COUNTY, Montana Territory, trailed the two rustlers out of the Two Bear Mountains, across the rolling prairie eastward, and into the Little Rockies.

He was out of his jurisdiction now, his second day out of Clantick, but he knew the Blaine County sheriff wouldn't mind. This was a big country, with counties as vast as some Eastern states, and if every sheriff gave up the owlhoot chase when said owlhoots crossed jurisdictional boundaries, the owlhoots would reign.

Besides, he was closing on these two. He could feel them slowing ahead of him, growing weary of the cat-and-mouse game they and Stillman had been playing ever since Stillman had come across the small herd they'd stolen from Bernie Beloit and his drover, Hector Sanchez—murdered with a bullet through his throat, his eyes eaten out by crows.

The murdering long-loopers had abandoned the cattle when they'd discovered Stillman was trailing them and hotfooted it east. They wouldn't be heading east much longer, though. A heavy-shouldered, middle-aged man in a blue chambray shirt, just over average height, with deep-set eyes, sun-leathered skin, and a big, bushy mustache, Stillman halted his bay on a sage-covered knoll, removed his Stetson, and ruffled his longish salt-and-pepper hair.

He was close. Damn close. The bandits had stopped and were not far away. Probably planning to ambush him, shoot him out of his saddle the way they'd shot Hector Sanchez. It made sense. If Stillman were on the run, only one man behind him, that was what he'd do.

Why run when there were plenty of places in which to affect a drygulching?

Stillman donned his hat as he stared eastward, running his dark-blue gaze along the low, pine-and-piñon-stippled bench about four hundred yards before him. The sun was too high and brilliant to detail the ridge, but Stillman could see the two sets of shod prints heading toward it, pocking the chalky, gravelly soil beneath his own horse and mean-dering out across the sagey flat toward the bench.

If it were later in the day, with the waning sun bringing details into relief, he'd no doubt see the two renegades snugged into the rocks atop that bench, aiming rifles at him. As it was, he had only his gut instinct, but an instinct groomed by years of man-hunting, first as a soldier in the War Between the States, then as a deputy U.S. marshal, and now as sheriff of one of the largest, remotest, wildest counties in Montana Territory, hugging the Canadian border—a haven for fugitive whites, renegade Indians, and everything in between.

No, they were waiting for him, all right. Stillman would have bet the farm on that. He reached over and patted the walnut stock of his Henry rifle for reassurance, then gigged the bay ahead and into a depression that took the bench out of sight—and himself out of sight from the bench.

He halted the bay, slipped out of the leather, and tied the horse to a low pine. The horse shook its lustrous black mane and rolled its eyes with annoyance.

"Sorry, Sweets," Stillman said. " I know you want to be in on the action, but I got a plan." He patted the horse's nose. "Bear with me, ole hoss."

Chuckling, Stillman walked around the hollow gathering small branches for a fire. When he'd gathered an armload, he set the wood down and formed a small ring with stones. Using crushed pine cones and dried leaves for tinder, he struck a match and built a flame.

He encouraged the fire with the smallest kindling, gradually adding larger until he had a blaze hot enough for boiling coffee. To this, he added several green cottonwood branches with the leaves attached. He fanned the fire with another leafy branch and watched the gray, eye-watering smoke billow up from the hollow, where it could be seen from the bench.

"Okay, Sweets," Stillman said, shucking his Henry from the saddle sheath. "Back in three jangles of a whore's bell." He chuckled. His lovely wife, Fay, always looked at him cross-eyed when he used the uncouth expression.

He the neck of the antsy horse, swung around, and trotted southward along the hollow, crouching so he wouldn't be seen from the bench. When he'd gone roughly a hundred yards along the base of the eastward-arcing swale, he climbed out and ran crouching across the brushy flatland, depending on his "cookfire" to divert the owlhoots' attention.

He could hear them in his mind's ear: "What the hell—he's stoppin' for *coffee?*"

At least, that was what he hoped they were saying, and believing. Otherwise, they might catch sight of him sneaking around them, and greet him on the bench with a lead storm.

He climbed the bench easily, hopping from stone to stone, his rifle in his left hand, his cocked Army .44 in his right—just in case. Making the crest of the bench and seeing no one around—just more buffalo grass and sage clumps and scattered junipers and pines, with prairie dogs laughing farther eastward—he relaxed, sheathing his Colt, sitting on a rock, and scrubbing the sweat from his forehead with the navy bandanna he wore around his neck.

Rested, he started northward along the bench, intermittently crouching behind shrubs, trees, and rocks, watching for the trail wolves.

Finally, after he'd walked a quarter mile, he came to a ravine rimmed with rocks. Peering over the side, he spied two horses tethered to an old cottonwood looming over a run-out spring, where the grass was deep and thick.

His heart tapping lively, Stillman licked his lower lip, scanning the area, then half-sliding on his butt lowered himself into the ravine. Watching the horses and moving carefully, trying not to frighten the tethered mounts, he walked northward through the brush, pushing through bull-berry and serviceberry clumps.

He climbed a knoll and stopped.

He scowled at the two men below—one leaning on a rock and staring westward down the bench, the other sitting on a driftwood log and doing the same. Both wore tattered trail clothes including chaps and run-over boots. The bandannas around their necks fluttered in the breeze. Six-shooters reclined in tied-down holsters, and both men were holding Winchesters.

Stillman didn't doubt that fresh brass was snugged in the rifles' chambers, awaiting his arrival.

No more than thirty feet from both men, and owning the higher ground, Stillman had the drop on them. He wanted to take them alive. Not that they deserved such consideration after what they'd done to Hector Sanchez and who knows how many more isolated stockmen, but Stillman knew it wasn't up to him to decide guilt or innocence. His job was to take these long-loopers to the judge, preferably alive.

"All right—hold it there, boys!" he ordered. 'Twitch and you're ghosts."

Both men stiffened, sun-seared cheeks bunching as they winced. Their heads turned slowly to the man behind them.

"I said don't move!" Stillman barked. "I've got the drop on you. There's no way out. Just lower those rifles and set them down slow. Then—and only then—turn around and face me. You so much as twitch before you've dropped those rifles, you're wolf bait."

"Same to you, Stillman. Drop that Henry or you're a dead man." The voice had come from behind Stillman, turning his blood to ice.

He stood frozen, staring at the backs of the other two men, his heart pounding. *Three* men? But he'd been following the sign of only *two*.

With no time to dawdle, and with the first two men starting to swing toward him with their rifles extended, Stillman twisted and dropped to his left knee. The man behind him fired a six-shooter, and the bullet whistled just over the top of Stillman's left shoulder. Lifting his Henry before the man could recock, Stillman quickly aimed at the man's chest and fired.

A split wink after his rifle had barked, Stillman threw

himself right and rolled as the two drygulchers fired their Winchesters in unison. They'd each fired one round and were jacking second shells into their chambers when Stillman, coming out of his second roll, planted himself on his elbows, bringing the Henry up with a shell already chambered, and fired.

Blood blossomed on the chest of the tallest of the two drygulchers, and he fell backward off his feet, his rifle firing skyward.

Just as the other owlhoot extended his rifle at Stillman, the sheriff rolled back to his left, jacking another round in the Henry and feeling the hot wind of the drygulcher's bullet whine past his head and hearing it spang off a rock two feet behind him. The gunman was jacking a shell into his own rifle when Stillman turned onto his elbows and extended the Henry.

Aiming calmly down the barrel, he fired a neat, round hole through the shooter's forehead. The man's chin jerked up, his arms dropping, the rifle falling. He shuffled backward two steps, his head canted back on his shoulders as if watching a high-flying bird. Then he stopped, dropped to his knees, and fell face down in a sage clump—deader than a hangman's soul.

Stillman found the third man's horse east, on the other side of a knoll, tethered in a cottonwood copse.

He conjectured the man must have been coming to meet the first two, figuring they had beef to drive—probably to an Indian agency or a remote roadhouse—and arrived at their preplanned meeting spot just in time to make Stillman's job woolly.

The sheriff retrieved the third horse, tied it with the others, collected what the three men were wearing on their persons, and stuffed it all in one of the three sets of saddlebags. Then he wrestled the bodies atop the horses, covered them with their bedrolls, and tied them to their saddles.

A half hour later he'd retrieved Sweets and was leading the three horses, tied tail to tail, southeast, toward the little town of Lone Pine.

He'd have preferred heading straight back to Clantick, where he knew his lovely wife worriedly awaited his return, as she always did when he was called away from town. But it was a warm June, and the bodies wouldn't last the two and a half days it would take him to ride that far. He'd ride the ten or so miles to Lone Pine, turn the bodies over to Marshal Charlie Boomhauer for burial in the town's boot hill, and head home tomorrow, he and his horse refreshed from a hearty supper and a good night's sleep.

Fay...

As he rode through the warm afternoon, he couldn't help thinking of her now, clad in the see-through wrapper she always wore when she wanted to make love, maybe pretending to be grading her school papers or preparing the next day's lesson plan. He'd go to her then, quietly, and lean down and nuzzle her neck, brushing her thick chocolate hair back from her ear and slipping a hand inside the wrapper, massaging her bosom until she sighed and leaned her head against his shoulder...

Scowling, he shook his head, glancing with frustration at the sky and the land sweeping around him. He was a long way from home—forty miles, at least. When he got to Lone Pine, he'd be about fifty miles from Fay—a two-day ride. No use torturing himself with lustful fantasies.

But, by God, when he got home...

He caught sight of Lone Pine a half hour later—the small, insignificant-looking village perched on a mountainside, the single pine after which it had been named looming on the rocky ridge behind. Following the mean-dering mail road up the slope terraced by shallow canyons and ravines and studded with pines and junipers, Stillman made the sleepy little village a few minutes later, the three horses and their grisly cargo lined out behind.

It was cooler up here in Lone Pine, high in the foothills, and the freshening breeze felt good, pushing under Stillman's sweaty collar and caressing his sunburned face. Pine smoke wafted from a cafe, tinged with the smell of cooking, and Stillman's stomach grumbled at the thought of a steak.

He'd been to Lone Pine a few times before, on similar missions, and had no trouble finding the little jailhouse set on the western edge of town, between Little Pine Creek and the livery barn. It wasn't much, just a little frame box with a shake roof, a sagging porch over which a fly-flecked shingle hung, TOWN MARSHAL burned into the front and back. Weeds and sage grew in the yard around the structure, where a single killdeer skittered along the ground, admonishing Stillman and feigning an injured wing.

"Oh, I don't want your nest, Mother," the sheriff assured the bird, reining the bay to a stop.

Dismounting, Stillman slip-knotted the horses to the tie rack and climbed the single step to the porch. He knocked on the plank door once, punched the latch, and entered the gloomy little office, stopping just beyond the threshold.

A big, raw-boned young man in a deer-hide vest was sitting behind the kitchen-table desk, kicked back in his swivel chair, dusty boots crossed on the desktop. He gave a start and glanced up with annoyance from the folded newspaper in his hands.

"Now what the hell...?" He stopped and scrutinized the dusty, unshaven stranger standing silhouetted in the open doorway.

"Who are you?" Stillman asked, beating the kid to the punch.

"Me?" the young man asked, tossing his newspaper onto the desk and dropping his feet to the floor, regarding Stillman curiously, apprehensively. "Why... I'm Nick Corey. Marshal o' Lone Pine."

Chapter Three

"WHO THE HELL ARE YOU?" THE YOUNG MAN ASKED Stillman as he climbed slowly to his feet, his gaze haughty and belligerent. With close-set, gray eyes, blunt nose, and weak jaw, he was Stillman's height, but he lifted up on his toes a little to make himself taller. He wore a weathered Stetson with a curled brim, and he carried a big Colt Dragoon in a low-slung holster.

Stillman reached into his shirt pocket and showed the kid his star, which he never wore while trailing, as it reflected sunlight. "Ben Stillman. I'm the Hill County sheriff out of Clantick."

"Oh," Corey said. His demeanor changed abruptly, turning sheepish. "I, uh ... I, uh," he hemmed and hawed, looking around as if searching for words.

"Where's Charlie Boomhauer? Don't tell me he retired."

"Well... no... he didn't retire, sorry to say," the young man said. "He, uh, well... Charlie died last week."

"Died?" Stillman's expression betrayed his shock. "What happened?"

"He, uh..." The kid pointed to the hide-covered chair on the other side of his desk. "You wanna have ye a seat there, Sheriff Stillman?"

Stillman shook his head with annoyance. "I've been sittin' all day. What in the hell happened to Marshal Boomhauer?"

The kid backed up, bent his knees, and fell back into the chair behind his desk, giving a long sigh, looking fidgety and flushed. "Well, last week," he said, sliding his enervated gaze around his desktop cluttered with illustrated magazines and playing cards, "we got a report on rustlers working the range south of here, back in the mountains. Ole Charlie rode out to check on it while I tended the shop—I was the deputy then, ye see—and... well, he never came back."

The kid paused. He ran his left index finger along the edge of the desktop.

"I went out that night lookin' for him. Found him too—with a bullet through his back."

Stillman flushed, frowning—surprised and grieved by the information. He hadn't known Boomhauer well—they'd teamed up on two short trips to track owlhoots haunting both Boomhauer's country and Stillman's—but Stillman had warmed instantly to the good-natured old cowpoke-turned-marshal. The man had been unassuming and self-effacing, but Stillman knew he had the kind of grit it took to be an effective lawman in these parts.

He couldn't believe the man was dead.

"Damn," he said, running a contemplative hand along his stubbly jaw, absorbing the information. "I'm... I'm sorry to hear that," he said, turning and staring pensively out the open door. "Charlie was a good man."

The deputy pursed his lips as he stared at the desktop, solemnly nodding his head. "Yes, he was," he whispered.

"He... well, damn... he taught me everything I know about being a lawman. Now, I know I prob'ly look pretty green to a man like you, Mr. Stillman, but by golly, I have to tell you, ole Charlie taught me how to handle saloon fights and just about everything else a lawman runs into around here. He taught me how to walk soft when you should, and when to march. By God, he taught me when to draw my gun and when to leave it in the holster and use words instead."

His voice had gradually increased with his passion. Now it softened again, and he shook his head. "Yessir, that man taught me everything I know, and I was still learnin' from him right up until the day he died."

He raised his gaze to Stillman, his eyes rheumy and direct. "He was like a father to me... the father I never had..."

Stillman had turned to the young man—the new marshal of Lone Pine—and was studying him critically. Deciding to withhold judgment, as this was no doubt a hard time for the lad, he nodded sympathetically.

Thoughtful, Stillman found a mug on the desk, turned to the stove, and filled the mug with coffee. He felt an angry burn in his gut—the kind of burn one lawman feels when he's heard another's been murdered.

"You haven't caught the killer I take it. Any idea who it is?"

"Nope."

"How come?"

"Just didn't have enough leads," the kid said with a fateful sigh. "The horse tracks gave out a few yards from the murder scene, and there were no witnesses, so..."

Corey lifted his hands and dropped them, palms down, to his knees. "I figured more rustling would be reported, and I'd go after the owlhoots and find Charlie's killer, but the mountains have been damn quiet lately. Not so much as a calf's disappeared."

"No strangers around town?"

"Nope."

"What about in the country?"

"Not a one. I figure whoever killed Charlie hightailed it and hightailed it for good. Damn the luck anyway." Corey sighed again and ran his index finger back along the edge of his desk. "But that's the way of it, though, ain't it, Sheriff? We lawmen never know when we're gonna take a stranger's bullet and end up crow feed--with no one to tell the tale."

Stillman stood by the stove, holding his coffee and regarding the young deputy, incredulous. "Don't tell me you've given up!"

Corey convulsed in his chair, sitting up straight. "Hell, no! No, sir! Why, every day I take a ride in the country, hopin' I'll hear or spot somethin' unusual, run across a stranger or two with runnin' irons or stolen beef." He shook his head sincerely. "No, sir. Nick Corey will not rest until he's found the killer of his hero, Charlie Boomhauer. No, sir..."

"Have you wired the lawmen in all the surrounding counties, asking about suspicious strangers and rustling problems?" Stillman knew he had not; at least, Stillman hadn't received any such wire. Hell, he hadn't even known Boomhauer was dead!

The young deputy looked up at Stillman, his eyes turning hard." Slowly, evenly, he said, "No, I reckon I haven't. But I will. And I thank you for the advice."

Knowing he'd offended the young man, Stillman said, "I didn't mean to tell you your job, son. It's just that Charlie Boomhauer was a good man, and he deserves to have his killer brought to justice. If you need any help—"

"If I need any help, I'll ask for it" the deputy inter-rupted, all trace of humor washed from his face. His jaw was hard, his eyes like flint "Now suppose you tell me what brought you to our humble little town, Sheriff."

Stillman studied the young whip, trying to get a read on just who he was and what he was about—a difficult task, he could see. The kid was wrapped tighter than the springs on a new hack. Stillman wondered if he was just young and defensive, with too much on his plate of a sudden, or... or what? Whatever he was, sitting here reading newspapers and magazines wasn't going to help him find Boomhauer's killer.

After taking a moment to remember what had brought him to town in the first place, Stillman said, "I have three dead men outside. Rustlers."

The sandy-haired Corey looked at Stillman hopefully. "Maybe they're the ones that murdered ole Charlie!"

Stillman shook his head. "I doubt it. They're part of a larger syndicate working over west and north. I've had my eye on them for the past two months. Finally caught 'em with beef on the move."

Corey winced, crestfallen, and rubbed his jaw. "You don't say..."

"They murdered a drover a few days back," Stillman continued. "I began following them then, took them down earlier today, northwest of here. Rather than trail them back to Clantick in this weather, I thought I'd drop them here for burial. Didn't figure Charlie'd mind. We've kind of worked together that way, last couple years."

Stillman noticed the lad staring at him, glassy-eyed.

"What are you lookin' at?"

Corey shook his head wonderingly, his eyes aglow with admiration. "I just can't believe I'm sittin' here in the pres-ence of the great Ben Stillman. Why you're famous—

don't you know that? Leastways, in Montana ye are. Why, when I was a kid, I used to read about you in the newspapers."

The Lone Pine marshal raised a hand in the air as though following a headline. "U.S. Deputy Marshal Ben Stillman Captures Kelly Gang in Raptor's Gulch! The Great Ben Stillman Single-Handedly Foils Bannack Bank Heist!" Corey slapped his hands together and gave a hoot. "Why, you were one of my heroes, growin' up--you know that?"

Stillman found himself once again staring at the young man, baffled by the kid's sudden change of tune. A more fickle nature he'd rarely encountered.

"I was sure sorry to hear about you takin' that bullet in the back down Virginy City way," Corey said.

"I appreciate your sympathy," Stillman grunted, finishing his coffee.

"Guess you're back in the saddle now, though, huh?"

"With a rather sore ass at the moment." Stillman set his empty coffee cup on the desk and started for the door. "I'm gonna turn these dead men over to you and your undertaker."

"Headin' home?"

Stillman thought he detected a hopeful note in the kid's voice. At the door, he turned around. "Tomorrow mornin'. My horse is tired, and so am I. I think I'll get a room and a bath, then pay my respects to Charlie's widow."

Stillman headed outside and retrieved a bulging set of saddlebags off one of the outlaw's mounts. He draped it over the tie rail.

"What are them for?" Corey asked, standing in the open doorway, both hands on the frame.

"Those are the saddlebags with these owlhoots' personal belongings—including their guns. I'll bring them back to Clantick with me, but in the meantime, you'll want to..."

"I know, I know," the lad said, his testiness returning. "Keep them under lock and key."

"Good man," Stillman said. He touched his hat brim and reined away from the hitchrack.

"You might think twice about seein' Mrs. Boomhauer," Corey called after him. "She's pretty broke up. No one but her neighbor's seen her since the funeral, and her shades are always down. Poor woman."

Without turning around, Stillman said, "I appreciate the advice, but a visit's only proper. I'll stop back in the morning for those saddlebags."

The tall, sandy-haired young man in the worn trail clothes—hat shoved back on his head, tin star on his stained vest—stood on the jailhouse stoop as Stillman rode over to the livery barn. Corey was grinning, squinting against the late afternoon light.

"The great Ben Stillman," he muttered under his breath.

He paused, watching Stillman approach the barn and dismount as the livery man, Dewey Seton, stepped out through the open doors. Corey was still grinning, his eyes on the sun-seasoned, yoke-shouldered Stillman, when he scratched his head and said, "I'm gonna kill 'em."

———

WHEN STILLMAN HAD DROPPED Sweets at the livery barn, he headed to the Maclean House, on the south side of Crawford Street. The tidy, two-story building with a grand, white portico sat across Lone Pine Creek, in a small grove of aspens rattling their leaves in the fresh, early-evening breeze. There was a buggy shed behind the place, as well as a log barn, which looked as though it hadn't been used in some years.

Toting his saddlebags on his left shoulder and his rifle in his right hand, Stillman stepped over the dozing dog on the porch and through the green-painted screen door.

"I'll be taking that rifle from ye, mister," said a stooped, wizened old man entering the parlor wearing green eyeshades and a blue serge coat that hung off his shoulders like a sack. "If'n you're wantin' a room here, that is."

"I'm wanting a room, all right," Stillman said, producing his sheriff's star from his pocket and tossing it on the register book lying open on the counter.

The old man squinted up from the badge. His brows were shaggy moth wings, obscuring his eyes. "Lawman?"

"Sheriff Stillman from Clantick. I'm here on business."

"Oh...I see," the old man said, paling slightly, a muscle working in his withered cheek. He turned the register on its revolving pedestal, dipped the pen, and offered it to Stillman, who took it and signed his name.

"I'm August Maclean. You here to investigate the marshal's murder?"

"No," Stillman said. "Just heard about it, as a matter of fact."

The man looked relieved. "Not much need, anyway. Our new marshal's on top of it."

"Is he?" Stillman asked skeptically.

"Why, sure! Ole Nick, he might look green, but Charlie trained him good!"

Trained him to sit around reading magazines, Stillman thought puzzled by the hotel keeper's comment. Most townsfolk would be so shaken by the murder of their marshal they'd welcome all the help in solving his murder they could get

"Well, I hope he gets his man," was all Stillman said.

"Oh, he will, he will." Old Maclean turned away, fetched a key off one of the gold hooks lined up behind him, and turned back, offering the key to Stillman. "Room seven. Take the stairs yonder. Last room on the right. Nice and private. Breakfast is served from seven to nine."

"Much obliged." Stillman turned and started for the stairs.

"Can I... can I ask ye how long you're stayin', Sheriff?"

The old man's mincing voice turned Stillman back around. "I'll be leaving at first light."

"Much obliged," Maclean said, spreading a grin and touching the visor of his eyeshade. His mood obviously enhanced, he said, "Hope ye enjoy your evening. We'll be servin' supper—my wife, our granddaughter, an' me—in the dining room yonder, in case you're interested."

The old man studied him, smiling over the register book, that muscle in his cheek still working.

"I'll be here," Stillman said. He started turning away but stopped as a thought occurred to him. "Can you tell me where Boomhauer's widow lives? I wanted to pay my respects later, but I forgot to get directions from Corey."

The glitter faded from the old man's eyes, and the muscles in his face tensed. He cleared his throat and wiped his nose, dropping his eyes for a sheepish moment to the desk on which his elbows were propped.

"Uh...she lives off Montana Avenue there...north of town. Little blue house behind the blacksmith shop. You'll see chickens and a horse pasture."

Stillman nodded. "Say, if I wanted to stay an extra day or two—you know, just to do a little snooping of my own —would I have to reserve a room now, or could I wait till tomorrow?"

The old man's face was parchment-pale as he studied Stillman darkly, his eyes brooding, his jaws working from side to side, like a horse chewing cud. "Well, now, I don't really think it's necessary you stayin' on, Marshal."

"Oh?" Stillman asked, vexed by the man's presumption. "Just the same..."

Dropping his eyes and making a show of studying the register book open before him and running a finger along a page, Maclean cleared his throat and said, "No... I guess we're not too busy this week. I reckon you could wait and let me know... uh, tomorrow. But please don't wait till the last minute!"

Stillman smiled. "Much obliged."

He climbed the stairs and found his room at the end of a long, dark hall. At the far end of the house, the room was indeed private, Stillman mused. There was a door adjacent to Stillman's room, and the sheriff walked to it and looked out.

White plank stairs dropped to the yard below, where a clothesline slumped under wet clothes, and two privies stood side by side, at the end of a brick path.

Stillman looked it over with a lawman's customary scrutiny, then entered his room and tossed his saddlebags and Henry rifle on the bed. Tired, he sat on the bed, tossed his hat aside, and ran his right hand through his hair.

It had been a long ride, and on top of everything else, he'd learned a good man was dead... murdered. He had a mind to stay on here and look into the killing himself, but then he thought of Fay and his own deputy, Leon McMannigle, waiting for him back home. There was also the fact that the new marshal here didn't want him around.

Stillman removed his shell belt and lay back on the bed and dozed for fifteen minutes. Then he got up, went to the washstand, and poured himself a glass of water. Looking in the mirror as he drank, he saw the three-day stubble and trail dust on his face.

Wanting to rid himself of both before heading over to Boomhauer's widow's place later this evening, he strapped his Colt Army around his waist, donned his hat, and left the room. He took the outside stairs to the yard, pushed through the damp wash on the line, and headed for the main drag, Crawford Street.

He strolled west along the boardwalk and pushed through the door of Tattersall's Barber Shop.

"Sheriff Stillman!" the man in the barber chair exclaimed with a start, lowering the newspaper he'd been reading.

About fifty, he was a jowly man with protruding blue eyes, jug ears, and thin blond hair combed over the bald crown of his skull. He wore a striped shirt with sleeve garters, and baggy, broadcloth trousers.

The three loafers sitting along the wall to Stillman's right, flanking a small, knee-high table covered with newspapers and a checkerboard, regarded the newcomer with wary surprise. The oldest, a wiry gent in his eighties and wearing a sheepskin vest in spite of the warm weather, said with a moronic gleam in his eye, "We was just talkin' about you!"

The jowly man climbed out of the barber chair and chastised the old gent with a look. He formed a taut smile as he looked at Stillman, and said with strained reserve, "We saw you ride into town, Sheriff. And, being the snoops we are, we were just wondering... uh..."

"Wondering who the dead men were," one of the loafers, a stalky man with a bushy red beard, finished for him.

"Longloopers from over west," Stillman said. "I doubt they had any connection to your marshal's murder—if that's what you're wondering."

With a somber, affable smile, Stillman hung his hat on

the tree beside the door and slid his glance around the room. The jowly man who'd been sitting in the chair said, "Yep, that's what we were wondering, all right. You heard about Charlie, I reckon. Damn shame, damn shame."

There was a grim silence. Then the jowly man extended his hand. "Marv Tattersall. What can I do you for this afternoon, Sheriff? Shave and a trim?"

"And a long, hot bath."

"The tub room is right this way," Tattersall said, heading for the room's back door.

Stillman followed the man, and in ten minutes he was scrubbing and soaking in a copper tub in a cedar-lined back room, the back door open to let out the steam and heat from the grumbling boiler.

When Stillman had dried and dressed, he headed back to the main room, where Tattersall was stropping a razor while two of the loafers played checkers and the third one, the old man, dozed with his chin on his chest.

"Have a seat, Sheriff!" the barber said, grinning broadly as he stropped the bone-handled blade. "You're about to enjoy the closest, most painless shave on the Hi-Line!"

Chapter Four

STILLMAN KNEW THE BEST PLACE FOR LEARNING A town's gossip was in its barbershop.

At least, he *had* known that. Now, however, he was beginning to wonder. The three loafers sitting to Stillman's left, smoking and chewing and spitting into the sandbox strategically positioned on the floor, in spitting range of everyone in the room, were as tongue-tied as virgin farm boys at a May Day hop.

For the twenty minutes Stillman had been sitting in the chair with Tattersall's clippers snipping at his hair and the man's bone-handled razor plowing the lather and three-day stubble from his jaw, the barber had been asking all the questions—everything from how the weather had been over Clantick way, to the price of beef, and from how Stillman had taken down the dead men he'd hauled to town, to how long the sheriff thought he'd be staying hereabouts.

When Stillman said he'd be leaving in the morning, the loafers cut sidelong looks at each other, and for a flicker of an instant, the razor stopped its rake down Stillman's left cheek.

Before Stillman could wonder at it, however, Tattersall began a long tirade against President Arthur.

Stillman was puzzled.

In most towns where there'd been a recent killing, the killing was almost all anyone talked about. Everyone including the parson and spangled women had a theory about what had happened. But here, in the tiny trail stop of Lone Pine, where its marshal had been murdered only a week ago, no one seemed to want to talk about anything but the weather and how long Stillman was going to remain.

While the barber prattled on about a bill the president was trying to get passed into law, Stillman cleared his throat and, intending to go ahead and drop the bucket in the well, asked, "Anyone here have any thoughts as to who killed Boomhauer?"

Silence.

The barber's hands stopped their motion.

Outside, wagons squeaked, and chickens fought over spilled grain in the street.

"I reckon not," Stillman groused in wonder.

"Well," the barber piped up. "I guess we all figured... we all figured Core... uh, Marshal Corey... had it all figured out..."

"Rustlers?" Stillman asked.

"Well, sure enough, rustlers!" the red-bearded man exclaimed. "Why, they're robbin' the range between here and the Milk River in the north and the Missouri in the south!"

Then Tattersall and the loafers were off and running on the rustling subject, leaving Boomhauer—and Stillman—in the dust. They didn't finish until the barber had finished trimming Stillman's hair and mustache. All brilliantined and pomaded and smelling like a snake-oil salesman, Stillman donned his hat, paid his bill, bade a good afternoon to the barber and loafers, and stepped outside. Peculiar. Damn peculiar, he mused, pulling the door closed behind him.

Looking across the street, he saw Nick Corey stepping out of the bank. Corey saw Stillman then too. Corey gave a little backward jerk, as though about to slip back inside the bank. But then the Lone Pine marshal realized Stillman had already seen him. He fashioned a big smile and waved a hearty arm above his head.

"Hello, Sheriff!" he called.

Stillman nodded, smiling wryly.

"Had ye a bath and a shave, I see," Corey called across the street

Stillman smiled again and fashioned an idiotic shrug.

Corey said, "Tattersall's a good barber. The best in the business, I've always said."

"I'd vouch for him," Stillman allowed.

Corey waited for a farm wagon to pass, then asked with an inquisitive frown, "Where you stayin' tonight if you don't mind me askin'?"

Stillman hesitated. "The Maclean House."

"Ah," Corey said with a nod. "Good place. Fewest bed-bugs in town." He laughed. "Well, busy, busy!" With that, the Lone Pine marshal hitched up his gun belt and crossed the side street, continuing down the boardwalk toward the jail.

Stillman stared after him. He didn't like that kid, and he wasn't sure why. Was it only because the young man obviously didn't want him around? Stillman guessed he could understand Corey's motivation for that. After all, finding Charlie's killer was the town marshal's job, on behalf of the county sheriff in this remote area. And having Stillman around might undermine his authority and make him look like a whelp before his town.

But then again, if it were Charlie, he and Stillman would be gassing over saloon beers about the problem, covering every angle, puzzling it over, talking it through.

Not this kid. He wanted Stillman out of town as fast as possible, and that just didn't jibe with the lawman's professional code...

Fishing his timepiece out of his shirt pocket, Stillman saw that it was nearly six o'clock. At last, he could quell the rumbling in his stomach. With that intention, he started back toward the Maclean House, crossing the creek as the westering sun turned the aspens buttery gold.

In the hotel's small dining room, three of the half-dozen tables were occupied. A blond girl of about seventeen and wearing a calico dress with a ruffled apron was taking orders and serving.

All faces turned for an instant toward Stillman as the sheriff made his way to a table. He nodded affably and sat down, and all eyes retreated.

The waitress disappeared through the swinging door into the kitchen and reappeared a minute later with two plates heaped with food. When she'd set the food before two middle-aged men dressed in homespun farm clothes, she removed a pad of paper from her apron pocket and approached Stillman's table, her smooth cheeks flushing timidly.

"What can I get you this evening, sir?"

Glancing up from the card on which two menu choices had been penciled, Stillman said, "That pork roast with all the trimmings sounds just what the doctor ordered. And coffee. Hot and black."

Scribbling on her pad, the girl nodded and disappeared into the kitchen again.

When the kitchen door opened a moment later, the wizened old hotel keeper appeared, glancing around the room. When his eyes found Stillman, they darkened. Flushing, Maclean ducked back into the kitchen.

Stillman frowned curiously, wondering what it was about him that upset the old man.

A few seconds later, the girl came out with a plate and a cup of coffee. She set the plate and coffee before Stillman without a word, then wheeled to answer a woman's request for more butter.

Stillman wolfed his food hungrily, aware of the furtive glances slid his way from nearly every table in the place. When he was finished with his food, he drained his coffee cup, then stood and left the room, heading for the privy out back.

When he returned a few minutes later, he saw that his plate had been removed, his coffee cup refilled. A corner of a folded slip of paper protruded from beneath the saucer. Taking his seat, he casually removed the slip and opened it

"Please meet me in the old barn behind the hotel at 9. Don't tell a soul." It had been scribbled in pencil on the back of a kitchen ticket

Stillman palmed the note and furtively stuffed it in the left hip pocket of his denims. He sipped his coffee and let his eyes prowl the room. One of the farmers glanced at him quickly and returned his gaze to his plate.

The waitress walked out of the kitchen, delivered a small dessert plate to a middle-aged businessman sitting alone in the corner, then strode to Stillman's table. Her gray eyes were cool.

"Can I get you some dessert this evening?"

Stillman studied her for a moment curiously. Then he smiled. "I'd love a slice of the peach cobbler."

"Coming, right up," the girl said affably and wheeled away.

The girl served the cobbler without meeting Stillman's gaze. When she'd refilled his coffee, she disappeared in the kitchen again.

Stillman glanced at her occasionally while he ate the pie, knowing it could have been only she who had left the message on his table. As he wondered what she wanted to talk to him about in so private a place as the old barn after dark, he felt his senses coming alive, his heart beating faster than before.

A few years ago, he might have thought the girl fancied him. But she was too young for him now, and besides, she didn't appear the type who would invite a man—young or old—into a dark barn for frolic. Of course, Stillman might be wrong. He'd known plenty of "upstanding" girls who had occasionally worked the dark side of the tracks for money, but this girl didn't appear that type.

No, she wanted to speak to him because she knew he was a lawman. To fully satisfy his curiosity, he knew, he'd have to wait until nine—a good two hours away.

In the meantime, he'd pay his visit—and one he was not looking forward to—to Charlie Boomhauer's widow.

———

"MRS. BOOMHAUER?"

"Yes?" From what Corey had told him about the grieving widow, he was surprised the woman even answered the door.

"I'm Ben Stillman, Hill County sheriff from over Clantick way."

"Oh. Yes. Charlie talked about you."

Stillman ran his fingers along the brim of his hat, which he held before him. He hesitated.

"Oh, where are my manners?" Mrs. Boomhauer asked. "Please come in, Sheriff."

The woman drew the door wide, and Stillman stepped into the dimly lit living room cozily furnished with braided rugs and oval photographs and daguerreotypes. There were two armchairs, a sofa, and a rocker upholstered with cowhide, its seat worn and cracked. A blue lamp sat on the table beside it, along with a stack of yellowed magazines, a folding-style, miniature chess set, and a corncob pipe resting in an ashtray.

On the floor beneath the table was a pair of well-worn, elk-hide slippers. Stillman hadn't known Boomhauer well, but his absence here was palpable. It resided too in the gray-haired woman who flavored Stillman with a wan smile as she closed the door softly and asked, "Would you like a cup of coffee, Sheriff? I have a pot warming on the stove."

"That would be nice," Stillman said. "I hope I'm not intruding."

"There's nothing to intrude on," Mrs. Boomhauer said tonelessly as she walked toward the kitchen—a kind-looking older woman with her coarse gray hair braided and wound in a tight bun. Slightly stoop-shouldered, she wore a brown wool sweater over a gingham dress, and soft-soled shoes that made little noise when she walked.

Stillman was surprised, after what Corey had told him, to have not only been let into the house but to have found not a frail, simpering, grief-stricken shell, but a stoic woman putting her best foot forward in spite of her loss.

"Have a seat anywhere," she called behind her.

"Thank you, ma'am," Stillman said, looking around awkwardly, still toying with his hat.

Mrs. Boomhauer returned with his coffee.

"It's funny," she said with an anemic half smile, taking a seat in the armchair across from Stillman and drawing her sweater about her shoulders. "We used to read about you, Charlie and I. When you were still a federal marshal."

"Oh."

"Yes, in the *Great Falls Tribune,* I guess it was. Charlie would find old copies in town and bring them home. That's when we were still ranching southeast of Lone Pine." Mrs. Boomhauer smiled again, listlessly. "He was proud to work with you after you became the sheriff of Hill County."

"Well, I was proud to work with him, ma'am," Stillman said. "The few times we worked together, that is. With Clantick and Lone Pine being fifty miles apart, I didn't have the honor that often. About twice was all. Even so, I've never worked with a better man."

"Thank you for saying so, Sheriff Stillman. Charlie's strutting with his chest out, I'm sure." She smiled at this and looked down at her own coffee, which she held on her lap.

Stillman flushed slightly and sipped from his cup.

Mrs. Boomhauer said, "He was a cowboy at heart, Charlie was. A cowboy with a badge. And sometimes I wish... now I wish... he'd just stayed a cowboy." Her brown eyes welled with tears, and her lips trembled. She set her chin in her hand, trying to steel herself. "I wouldn't have loved him any less."

Her voice broke, and she sobbed once. Composing herself, she brushed the tears from her cheek with the back of her hand.

Stillman looked away.

"I'm very sorry, ma'am, for your loss. If there's

anything I can do to ease your pain, I hope you'll let me know."

He knew how automatic the words sounded, but he didn't feel automatic at all. He felt sad and dull and not equal to the task of comforting this woman, who would no doubt spend the rest of her life in this little, ramshackle house alone.

Alone here with Charlie's empty chair, and his slippers beneath the table.

"No, there's nothing," Mrs. Boomhauer said, producing a handkerchief from her sweater and wiping her nose. "There's nothing... aside from catching Charlie's killer, that is, Mr. Stillman."

Stillman sighed. "Well, I reckon I'd feel honored to help as best I can, but this isn't my territory, ma'am. Besides that, it sounds like Nick Corey thinks it's some owlhoot that's drifted out of the country."

Still wiping her nose, Mrs. Boomhauer looked at Stillman peculiarly. "You mean a Gypsy, don't you? Someone from that band of Gypsies camped out in the mountains?"

"Corey never mentioned anything to me about Gypsies. He said it was rustlers."

"Yes, well, he probably meant the same thing," Mrs. Boomhauer said. "He thought Charlie found the Gypsies rustling stock out on Snaketrack range, and that's why they killed him. He thinks they've moved onto Canada by now."

Stillman's forehead creased once again. "He told me he thought the killer had headed south."

"Maybe it was south," Mrs. Boomhauer corrected herself, distracted. "I've been confused these past few days..."

Stillman nodded thoughtfully as he sipped his coffee.

"Do you have a wife, Mr. Stillman?"

"Yes, ma'am, I sure do."

"I bet she misses you when you're away."

"I reckon she does, ma'am, but not half as much as I miss her."

"I guess you'll be going back to her soon."

"Tomorrow," Stillman said with a nod, feeling awkward, knowing that Mrs. Boomhauer was pondering the prospect of never seeing her husband again.

Stillman and the widow talked for another half hour, in a desultory way, and Stillman drank another cup of coffee. When he'd drained his cup for the second time, he set the cup and saucer on the couch beside him and took up his hat.

"Well, I best be going, ma'am. Before I do, is there anything I can do for you around the place? Any heavy work needing done?"

"Oh, no, Sheriff. Thank you, though. I—" She appeared to think of something.

"What is it, ma'am? Please," Stillman urged.

"Well," she said slowly. "I—I do need some kindling

for the morning. Charlie used to do all the chopping in the morning before he left for work... I haven't hired a boy yet."

"Show me to the woodpile," Stillman said.

In the backyard, by lantern light, Stillman removed his hat and gun and split enough kindling for a week. He carried it all into the house and filled the kindling box beside the kitchen stove. When he was finished, he donned his hat and gun, bade the grateful widow good evening, and left by the front door.

'Thanks again, Mr. Stillman," Mrs. Boomhauer called after him.

"My pleasure, ma'am," Stillman said, half-turning and waving as he walked out of the yard, moving slowly until his eyes had adjusted to the darkness relieved by a rising moon.

As he walked, his mind shuttled back and forth between two questions: Why had Corey tried to keep him from visiting the widow, and why hadn't he told Stillman about the Gypsies?

Corey...

Why did questions keep popping up about the new marshal of Lone Pine?

Deciding he might be spending an extra day here after all Stillman quickened his step. Passing a giant pile of logs someone had no doubt hauled out of the mountains for firewood, he headed through a vacant lot, making a beeline for the jailhouse, to have a little visit with Lone Pine's distinguished peacekeeper.

He was halfway across the vacant lot when a woman's shrill cry pierced the quiet summer night.

Chapter Five

STILLMAN'S HAND SLAPPED HIS GUN GRIPS, BUT he kept the .44 in its holster. Frozen, he watched a buggy bounce out of the shadows on his right, heading south toward Crawford Street. It was a high-wheeled two-seater with a tasseled canopy and a black thoroughbred in the traces.

The driver, an older gent wearing a bowler, slapped the reins urgently while a young woman slumped in the seat beside him, wrapped in a white sheet or blanket.

Watching from the shadows, Stillman was curious. When the buggy had passed, he followed it turning left on Crawford Street and jogging a block east. At the livery barn, he stopped and looked toward the mercantile.

The buggy sat beside the mercantile building, its polished leather gleaming in the moonlight. The driver lifted the sheet-wrapped girl out of the buggy and hurried toward a staircase that climbed the side of the store.

On the top landing, a door opened, and a man appeared. Peering over the rail, he removed the pipe from his mouth and called in a faint British accent, "Wilfred, what is it?"

"She's bleeding again!"

The man on the stairs made an indecipherable exclamation and, the pipe in his mouth lumbered down the steps anxiously.

"I got her!" the man carrying the girl carped.

The other man turned, lumbered back up the steps, and disappeared through the door, leaving it open behind him. Wheezing from exertion, the man carrying the girl made the top of the stairs, jostled sideways through the door, and kicked the door closed with a shudder and a tinkle of vibrating glass. A dim lamp shone in the window in the door's upper half.

Stillman watched it for a moment wonderingly, then lowered his gaze to the shingle jutting over the boardwalk at the bottom of the stairs: LOWELL PERCIVAL, M.D.

Curious, but deciding the medical emergency had nothing to do with him, Stillman continued toward the jailhouse. The squat building was dark, but Stillman knocked anyway. When he'd pounded several times and received no answer, he turned away, frustrated.

He'd really wanted to talk to Corey, find out why the new town marshal hadn't mentioned anything about the Gypsies. Not that it was any of Stillman's business, but he'd been a lawman long enough to have developed a keen nose for trouble. He'd ask his questions as delicately as possible, careful not to step too hard on the defensive Corey's toes.

Corey might have been making his night rounds, or was camped out in one of the two saloons, Stillman decided. He walked up one side of Crawford Street and down the other, checking out both watering holes—the Wide Open and the Stockmen's. In both places, he found only a handful of bleary-eyed cowhands, sporting girls with the midweek yawns, and sallow-faced bartenders. The raucous piano music in the Stockmen's was a lame attempt to build a party out of scraps.

No Corey.

Outside the Wide Open's buttery windows, Stillman checked his watch. Eight fifty-five. Surely Corey hadn't turned in for the night. Stillman doubted he'd named a deputy yet, which meant, if he did his job right, he'd have to keep an eye on the town himself, at least until the saloons closed.

Stillman considered taking a table in the Wide Open and waiting for the deputy to make his rounds, but then he remembered he was supposed to meet the girl at nine and headed toward the hotel.

On the bridge across the creek, he paused to light the cigarette he'd been thoughtfully rolling while he walked. He retrieved a match from his pocket, but, trying to light it on his thumbnail, he dropped it

He stooped to pick it up, and from the corner of his right eye saw an orange flash. A revolver snapped. The bullet whistled over him, and he could feel its wind on his ear. Instinctively, he dropped to his side and rolled, clawing his .44 from his holster.

There was another pistol report on his left flank, then another on his right, both shots rending the darkness where his head had been before he'd dropped the match.

He aimed at the first muzzle flash and fired twice. Aiming at the second, he fired twice more. Then he rolled to the side of the bridge and dropped feet-first into the creek with a splash.

Crouching in the darkness, water pushing against his ankles, he waited. When thirty seconds had passed, and he'd heard nothing but a night bird's cry and the water tinkling over the rocks, he waded slowly across the creek and peered over the bank.

It was too dark to see anything but the silhouettes of the cottonwoods, their branches stirred by a breeze. Finally, he picked up a stone and lobbed it several feet to his left, skipping it off the bank.

Both ambushers fired simultaneously, one flash appearing twenty feet to Stillman's left, the other about thirty feet straight out. Wheeling to his left, Stillman fired once, then loosed another round straight into the trees before him. Ducking behind the bank, he reloaded quickly.

Feet thumped away through the weeds.

Stillman slapped his cylinder shut and bounded up the bank. Crouching, gun extended, he looked around and saw a shadow flickering in the starlight, bulling through the trees and brush toward Crawford Street.

He took two steps forward, dropped to a knee, extended the .44, and fired once. He looked through the smoke webbing in the darkness, then stood and ran. When he'd cleared the trees and saw the back of a store on Crawford Street, he moved slowly, gun extended, casting glances to his right for the other bushwhacker.

He was approaching a lean-to stock shelter, a wagon parked beside it when a gun flashed from the front of the store. The gun barked as the bullet slammed into the iron-rimmed wagon wheel, spraying iron shavings and lifting an angry *clang!*

Crouching, Stillman fired two shots at the muzzle flash, then ran to the back of the store. He peered around the corner. Cautiously, he stepped out from behind the store and was sidestepping toward some barrels when he heard footsteps in the weeds behind him.

The man had gone around the other side of the building.

Stillman dropped to a knee and hunkered with his back to the barrels, and the Colt Army held out and slightly up.

He waited.

Finally, the dark outline of a hatted head appeared around the corner and froze. Knowing the man would have a hard time seeing him against the barrels, Stillman waited, wanting only to wing him if he could.

Suddenly the man bolted around the corner, starlight flashing off the gun in his hand. Stillman aimed at the man's shoulder and fired. The man groaned and stumbled.

"Stop!" Stillman yelled.

But then he saw the moonlight on the gun barrel arcing toward him, and he fired twice more, knocking the man backward off his feet. The man gave several guttural grunts and half moans, and then fell silent

"Crap," Stillman said under his breath.

He walked to the man through the wafting powder smoke and was about to kick the revolver away from the body when a familiar voice behind him said, "Hold it right there! Don't move!"

"Hold on, Nick. It's me—Stillman."

Corey didn't say anything, and Stillman stood there, hands spread acquiescently, half expecting a bullet. Something told him one of the two ambushers had been Corey. Why he didn't know. But he didn't know why the man hadn't wanted him to visit with Boomhauer's widow and hadn't told him about the Gypsies, either.

Someone called from up the street, "Hey, what's goin' on over there?"

Stillman turned his head and saw several silhouettes on the boardwalks on both sides of the street a half block away. Customers from the saloons, no doubt, who'd heard the shooting and come out for the show.

"That's what I aim to find out!" Corey yelled to them. "Go on back inside. Everything's under control."

Stillman watched the two crowds hesitate, then slowly drift back through the batwings on both sides of the street. He was glad they'd shown up. He had a feeling that if there hadn't been any witnesses, he'd be minus a heartbeat about now.

"Well, Stillman," the Lone Pine marshal said caustically. "What the hell's all the shooting about?"

"Ask him," Stillman said, jerking a thumb at the dead man.

Corey walked around Stillman and looked down. He whistled. "Hell's bells. You sure snuffed his candle."

"There was a second shooter. You wouldn't know anything about him, would you?"

"How would I know anything? And what makes you think you can ask *me* questions? You're the one just killed a man—in my town."

Stillman saw Corey's big Dragoon aimed at his belly.

"Haul your hands up, Stillman," Corey said sneeringly. "I'm takin' you in."

"All right, take me in, Nick," Stillman said, calling his bluff. "And then we'll have to call the county sheriff in from Chinook, and the circuit judge, and get a hearing. And then we'll find out why this man and the other one were shooting at me in the dark, and who was giving the orders... and why."

Corey stood there with his heavy Colt aimed at Stillman's belly. Stillman could hear the young marshal breathing through his nose, frozen as if in a block of ice.

Finally, Corey exhaled loudly and depressed his revolver's hammer, lifting the barrel and dropping the gun in his holster. He laughed.

"I reckon it wouldn't make sense, a reputable lawman

like yourself killin' a man in cold blood. Sorry about that. I guess I'm still a little green behind my ears—errin' on the side of caution, you might say."

"Mind if I check your gun to see if it's been fired recently? Just so I can rule you out."

Corey looked at the gun in his holster, then at Stillman. He laughed again, artificially. "You got a damn suspicious nature, Sheriff. You think I'm the other man?"

"Where were you five minutes ago?"

"Asleep in one of the cells. I always take a nap this time of the night, so I'm fresh when the saloons get to hoppin' later."

"I pounded on your door a few minutes ago."

"So I sleep sound. I'll work on it."

No longer worried about hurting the marshal's feelings,

STILLMAN ASKED, "Why didn't you tell me you suspected Gypsies of murdering Boomhauer?"

"'Cause I got to thinkin' on it later, and I decided it could have been anybody—Gypsies, Injuns, or white men." Corey sighed and shook his head. "Getta load o' you ... comin' down on me like you owned the whole damn county!"

Stillman watched him darkly, trying to read him, but there was no one more unreadable than Nick Corey. Then he squatted to appraise the dead man who lay on his back, arms spread, moonlight reflected on his slitted eyes and sandy hair. His hat lay a few feet away. He was dressed like a drover. A long, serpentine scar ran down the left side of his neck.

"You recognize him?"

Corey hunkered down near Stillman and looked at the dead man. "Well, now come to think of it, I do.

Clawson's his name. Bert, I think. He rode for Mr. Crawford."

"Crawford?"

"Max Crawford. Out to the Snaketrack. Don't that beat all! I wonder why Clawson was after you. He was a hardcase I know that. Maybe you arrested him one time, he seen you in town and decided to take you down. Or maybe he had some warrants on him that I didn't know about, but he thought you did. Hell, maybe he thought he was the reason why you were here! To track him down! He decided to beat you to the punch!"

Corey turned to the dead man and shook his head in awe. "We lawmen never know when we're gonna take a stranger's bullet and end up crow feed—no one to tell the tale. Do we, Sheriff?"

Tired of Corey's crap, Stillman stood up. "Tell me about the Gypsies."

Corey stood too and shrugged. "Well, they were camped out south of town for about six or seven months. Practically had 'em a little village out there. They traded with the farmers and ranchers in the area. Did a little rustlin' on the side. Well, Mr. Crawford found proof of it, and that's when Charlie went out to have a look around."

"Why didn't you mention them before?"

"'Cause it ain't your investigation."

He had him there, Stillman knew.

"I don't suppose you'd mind if I went out had a look around where Charlie was murdered?"

"Oh, man!" Corey complained, like a kid called in for bedtime, shaking his head and kicking at a brush clump. "You just don't give up do you?"

Stillman didn't say anything.

Finally, Corey said, "All right, all right. I'll show you out there tomorrow."

"I'd rather go alone. Why don't you draw me a map?"

"Don't trust me? Still think I'm the second shooter?"

"I work best alone."

"All right," Corey said with a nod. "All right. Come on back to the jail, and I'll sketch you a map." Glancing at the dead man, he said, "I'll send for the undertaker later."

Ten minutes later, both men stepped out of the jail. Stillman was folding the map Corey had sketched.

"Well, I best go wake the undertaker," Corey said. "Be seein' you, Sheriff."

"Be seein' you."

"Oh, and you be careful out there in them mountains tomorrow. That's a big empty country out there, and like I said before—"

"I know, I know," Stillman said. "We lawmen never know when we're gonna turn crow bait."

"With no one to tell the tale..." the marshal of Lone Pine added casually, walking away.

Chapter Six

STILLMAN STOOD IN THE DARKNESS OUTSIDE THE jail and watched Corey walk away, the back of the young man's vest glinting in the moonlight. Stillman scrubbed his jaw, then leaned against an awning post and slowly, thoughtfully rolled a smoke, carefully going over the recent events.

He didn't normally jump to conclusions, and he didn't think he was jumping to one now, deciding that the second shooter had indeed been Nick Corey. There was too much evidence pointing Corey's way, including the young man's perplexing attitude, and the fact that Stillman hadn't been able to find him earlier. Also, the young man had refused to let Stillman check his gun.

Stillman lit the quirley, inhaled deeply, then pushed off the awning post, heading across the street, angling south toward the hotel. When he came to the cottonwoods along the street, he pricked his ears and kept the coal of his cigarette cupped in his palm. He doubted anyone else would try to ambush him again tonight, but it paid to be careful.

The moon was high now, and nearly full. It silvered the leaves of the breeze-brushed cottonwoods and muted the starlight. The smell of pine drifted down from the ridges surrounding the town. In the distance, coyotes yipped. A dog on the other side of town howled a plaintive answer.

When Stillman was through the trees and standing at the edge of the Maclean House yard, he turned and looked back through the trees at the business district, with its false fronts silhouetted against the milky-dark sky.

It was such a small, quiet town, he thought, for the size of the secrets it kept.

Standing there, smoking the last of the cigarette, Stillman wondered about the girl the man had brought to the doctor. That reminded him of the girl he was supposed to meet at nine.

Quickly, he pulled his watch from his pocket, checked the time. Thirty minutes past.

He dropped the cigarette in the gravel, glanced at the few lighted windows in the hotel, deciding he hadn't been seen, then quietly made his way around the yard to the barn out back.

The moon cast the yard in deep shadows, making it difficult to see. Keeping his guard up, Stillman released the thong over the hammer of his .44 and made his way past the privy in the dew-damp grass, past a flowering lilac by the well pump, to the barn, which stood about seventy yards behind the hotel.

The grass was high around the barn, and the old implements abandoned there. Stepping through the grass, Stillman felt the dew collecting on his jeans. Pigeons made their worbling inquiries in the open loft doors.

"Hello, the barn," he said as he entered the dank building smelling of rotting wood, hay, and mouse droppings.

He stood just inside the door and to one side, so as not to outline himself in the frame. He fished a lucifer from his shirt pocket and scraped it to life on his thumbnail. "Hello?"

The ceiling was low, and mice scuttled in the loft. Shadows canted this way and that. A bird took flight from a beam and flew out the back.

"Anyone here?"

No reply.

Stillman waved out the match and tossed it out the door, into the dewy grass, where it sizzled softly in the silence.

For a half hour, he waited, sitting on a feed bin. Then he walked back around the hotel and entered by the front door.

"You almost got locked out," old Maclean said. He was sweeping the floor in front of the desk. "I lock up at ten."

Stillman didn't say anything. He looked around at the carpeted lobby lit by bracket lamps and into the dining room, where chairs had been placed upside down on the tables. He didn't see the girl.

With a nod to the old man, he crossed to the stairs, and was two steps up when the old man asked, "You stayin' tomorrow?"

"Yep."

Stillman went into his room and lit a lamp. He stripped down to his summer underwear and washed at the basin. After drinking a tall glass of water, he turned the covers back and slipped into bed. He piled the two pillows up behind him and crossed his arms over his chest, lying pondering for a long time, trying to figure out why the girl hadn't met him in the barn.

He didn't like being away from Clantick or Fay, but he had a feeling he'd remain here for another day or two.

The girl had a secret to tell, and he was going to find out what it was.

Someone had tried to kill him, and he was going to learn why.

————

"EVENIN', Mr. Drake," Corey said.

He'd been waiting in the yard of the big, brick house down the hill north of town, when the buggy swung into the yard, its leather shining in the moonlight He was smoking a cigar.

Drake stopped the buggy beside Corey. Alone in the two-seater, he too was smoking a cigar—the same brand of stogie Corey had. Both cigars were from the fragrant box Drake kept in his office at the bank.

"I knocked, but no one answered," Corey said, casting a glance behind him at the house, where only one third-story window was lit.

"I heard the shooting," Drake said. "Was that you?"

"Yep."

"You get him?"

"Nope. He got Clawson."

Drake didn't say anything for five seconds. Then softly he said, "Crap."

"It was Clawson's fault," Corey said. "He moved too fast. You shoulda just sent me."

"Does he know you were in on it?"

"Yeah, but he can't prove it."

"Does he know about Clawson?"

"I had to tell him he worked for Crawford. He would have found out for himself, one way or another. I told him Clawson was probably working on his own, though."

They talked for a while longer, then Corey asked, "How's Miss Sybil, Mr. Drake?"

"She's spending the night at the doc's," Drake grumbled, climbing out of the buggy. "Not feeling well, but never mind about her." He walked over to Corey and looked up at the taller man from under the brim of his crisp bowler, his spectacles flashing in the moonlight.

"Maybe you can put my horse and buggy to bed without fouling that up too." His voice was low, but it lashed like a whip.

"I told you, Mr. Drake—"

"I know what you told me. Now I'm telling you to put the buggy away and get the hell out to the Snaketrack and tell Crawford what's going on with Stillman. Then you remain in town and stay out of trouble until I tell you otherwise. Understand?"

Corey didn't say anything. He walked over to the big chestnut hitched to the buggy.

"Corey," Crawford snapped. "I asked you if you understood."

"I understand, Mr. Drake," Corey said tightly, not turning around. He took the horse by its bridle and started leading it to the dark shed sitting catty-corner to the house.

Drake stared after him, puffing his stogie. Then he turned through the gate and headed for the house, glancing at the one lighted window in the third-story gable, where a lone shadow paced.

———

WHEN NICK COREY rode back from the Snaketrack Ranch, his horse was nearly dead. He turned him over to Dewey Seton at the livery barn, then walked to the small house he rented on the northeast corner of town. It was nearly three in the morning, and the moon was down, the stars bright on the tin roofs of the shanties surrounding him in the darkness.

He stepped onto the porch, tried the knob. Locked. He pounded on the door.

"Open up, damnit. Open up, Biloxi. It's me—Nick. Open the damn door before I break it down!"

Finally, a light came on, the curtain in the door window was brushed aside, and the door opened. A slight brunette stood there sleepily in a pale blue housecoat; her face paint smudged.

"Nicky, where you been? It's so late." Her tired voice had a frog in it

Corey looked around the sitting room with its cheap, mismatched furniture, much of which had come with the house, some of which the brunette, Biloxi, and her sister, Florence, had rescued from trash heaps behind saloons and brothels. The faded paper on the walls was a floral pattern. Where it was missing, newspapers had been tacked up. There were no pictures on the walls. The air reeked of rotten food, whiskey, and stale cigarette smoke.

Corey noted the playing cards on the couch and on several tables, the empty glasses and bottles, and the overflowing ashtrays.

He looked at Biloxi. "You two ain't been entertainin', have you?'

Biloxi shrugged. "Flo's old beau was in town, and some friends."

"And some friends," Nick growled, studying the overweight Flo Kavanaugh passed out on the sofa, one arm flung over her face, her long, stringy hair tangled and matted. An empty bottle lay beside her on the floor.

She made little whimpering noises, dreaming.

"What's she doing here?" Nick demanded. "I got her a

room over at the boardinghouse. Still, she's always over here..."

"Mrs. Fredrickson threw her out again, Nicky."

"Why?"

"They don't get along. You know how Mrs. Frederickson is." Biloxi rubbed her eyes.

Cursing, Nick shut the door and stepped over the clutter on the floor to the kitchen, where he removed his gun belt and tossed it among the dirty dishes on the table. He ripped off his shirt, tossed it on a chair, and began pumping water into the basin.

"Did you have a hard day, sweety?" Biloxi asked, leaning against the table, arms crossed.

Corey only grunted as he splashed water on his face. He was thinking how much he'd like to put a bullet in Drake's left eye. Then he'd put one in his right eye, but only after he'd blown both the old man's knees off, and Drake had crawled around, begging Corey for his life.

Corey didn't like taking orders. Most of all, he didn't like being anyone's puppet. Damn grocery boy—that's what he was to Drake.

And now that Stillman had come to town, sniffing around in things that weren't his business... making Corey's life complicated. When all he'd wanted was to be the town's marshal and have people look up at him instead of down their noses for a change...

"Hey, what are you doing?" Corey asked as Biloxi walked up behind him and put her arms around him, pressing her face against his back.

"I just missed you, Nicky, that's all. Momma missed her daddy-man."

"If you missed me so damn much, why don't you fix me somethin' to eat. I'm damn near starvin' here. Work my tail off for you and that worthless sister of yours."

"Eggs all right?"

"Yeah, eggs are all right. Scramble me a bunch. I'm hungry. Been ridin' across the damn county, doin' more of Drake's dirty work."

Corey was drying his face briskly with a kitchen towel. Cursing, he tossed the towel on the table and sat down. He picked up a bottle, held it to the lantern light and scowled. He finished the whiskey and tossed the bottle into the trash box beside the door.

"Damnit!" he yelled. "How come when I come home the whiskey's always gone?"

In the other room, Florence whimpered loudly in her sleep.

"Shh, Nick, you'll wake Flo," Biloxi said, opening a cabinet door. She grabbed a bottle from the cupboard and, with a smile, set it on the table before Corey. "Here, Nicky. Look what Momma's got for her daddy-man."

Corey studied the label. "Applejack."

"Daddy's favorite!"

"Where in the hell did you find applejack around here?"

"Flo's old beau brought it. Said to give it to you."

Corey looked at the slight, rumpled girl suspiciously. "He did, did he?"

"Sure, he did, Nick." Biloxi turned back to the range where she'd begun cracking eggs into a skillet.

Corey popped the cork and smelled the lip. "Wonder what he wants."

"Why, he just wants to be your friend, Daddy."

"He wants to be my friend," Corey grumbled. "He wants to sell whiskey on the reservation—that's what Toby Blue wants. I know Toby Blue. He and I go way back..."

Corey laughed bemusedly. He took a swig and brought the bottle down, frowning and smacking his lips. "He sure does have a nose for liquor, though." He looked at the girl sleepily cracking eggs into the bacon fat popping in the skillet. "Billy, where did he get this stuff?"

"Didn't say," Biloxi said. "Just said it was for you, and he wouldn't let his friend or neither Flo or me have a taste. Said he wanted you to have it all."

"Said he wanted me to have it all," Corey mocked. "Well, next time he's in town, he better bring me more o' this, or he's gonna have a hell of a time around Lone Pine. I'm the town marshal now. Cock o' the walk."

Corey took another long pull from the applejack, getting his strength back, feeling plucky. He set the bottle down and kicked Biloxi's bottom, slamming her against the range. "Hey, how's my momma-girl anyway? She miss her daddy-boy?"

He grabbed her by her wrapper and yanked her onto his lap. She gave a startled squeal as he pawed her and nuzzled her neck.

"Oh, Nicky, your face is all scratchy!"

"How 'bout it, Momma? You miss your Nick-boy?" With a whoop, Corey picked the girl up and threw her over his shoulder like a sack of grain.

"Nicky! No! The eggs're gonna *burn!*"

Laughing, Corey carried the girl through the living room and into the bedroom and threw her on the bed. "Eggs can keep, Momma. Your Nicky-boy—he can't."

Twenty minutes later, Corey sprawled naked across the width of the mussed bed. He lay on his side, propped on an elbow, and he was twirling his revolver in his right hand thoughtfully. The angry glitter had returned to his eyes.

The girl gave her throat a timid clearing and got up.

She pulled a wrapper around her naked, chafed body, and
stepped to the door.

Quietly, she said, "I—I best go throw the eggs out."

"Yeah, you best do that, Momma. Then get your ass back here. I ain't finished with you yet."

Chapter Seven

STILLMAN WOKE EARLY THE NEXT MORNING, before dawn, and took a long stroll through town, just walking and thinking. He wondered if he was being fool-ish, not sending a wire to the Blaine County sheriff, whose jurisdiction this was, for help.

But then, he didn't have any hard evidence the town marshal had been involved in a crime. All he had was a feeling, and he didn't want to drag Melvin Bergquist all the way over here from Chinook on a hunch. He'd wait and see what turned up today.

He'd returned to his room and was shaving in the mirror over the washstand when a key rattled in the door. Reflexively, he drew his Colt, extending it, sighting down the barrel, as the door opened and the girl from the dining room gasped.

"Oh! My!"

Stillman quickly holstered his gun. "Sorry, miss, but have you heard of knocking? That's where you pound on a door before opening it."

The girl's eyes were wide, and her cheeks blushed red.

"I... I thought...!" She turned quickly and shut the door. She faced him and whispered, "I thought you were dead."

"What made you think that?"

"I heard all the shootin' last night, and..."

"And you knew it was meant for me?" Stillman blinked at her curiously. He stood there in his undershirt, his face half-shaved, his razor in his left hand.

A guarded looked suddenly crossed the girl's features, and she dropped her gaze to the thunder mug beside the bed. "I best empty your night pail for you. I'll wait till after you've left to make your bed."

"I'm not leaving today," Stillman said, watching her skeptically. She picked up the thunder mug by its wire handle and turned for the door.

"Hold on, hold on," Stillman said. "It was you that left the message on my table last night, wasn't it?"

She stopped and shook her head, fearful. "Please, Mr. Stillman. I don't want...I don't want him after me or my family."

"Who?"

The girl said nothing...

Stillman dropped the razor in the basin and wiped the lather off his face with a towel. He sat on the bed and took the girl's right hand in his. "Who? Is it Corey?"

She studied him warily and shook her head. "No. I mean, I reckon it is in a way, but... but I was gonna tell you about the Gypsies and"—she looked down—"my friend."

A man's gruff voice rose from the hall. "Rachel? Rachel, where are you? You've got potatoes to peel in the kitchen, girl."

Rachel turned and yelled, "Coming, Gramps!" To Stillman, she said, "I have to go," and headed for the door. At the door, she stopped and said, "Please just leave here, Mr. Stillman. It's best for all of us in Lone Pine."

Then she slipped out the door and clicked it closed behind her.

Later, Stillman had breakfast in the dining room. The girl served his eggs and potatoes and coffee without making eye contact When he'd finished and was crossing the lobby to the door, the old man scowled with frustration, and shook his head.

"Coming back?"

"Bet on it," Stillman said, donning his hat and stepping outside.

When he was sure no one was tracking him or laying for him in the cottonwoods along the creek, he fished Corey's map from his shirt pocket and studied it as he walked. He followed the route carefully with his eyes, noting the landmarks, wondering if the X really marked the place where Boomhauer had been murdered. Stillman had a feeling it didn't He'd check it out anyway. He might find out something. If someone tried drygulching him again, he'd know for sure that Lone Pine's marshal had his hand in something smelly.

And he'd keep an eye peeled on his backtrail.

As he approached the livery barn, he saw the livery-man, Dewey Seton, currying a roan pony in the paddock between the livery barn and the jail. Stillman nodded to the man and went into the barn, where he found Sweets in a stall near the front.

He talked to the bay, patted his rump, and bridled him. It was only after he'd tightened the belly strap and was adjusting the left stirrup that he saw the horse favoring its right rear hoof.

"What's the matter, boy?"

Stillman walked around behind the horse and lifted its hoof, clamping the forelock between his knees. The shoe was cracked.

Stillman frowned. That hadn't happened on the trail, because he would have noticed Sweets favoring that hoof. It had to have happened after Stillman had turned the horse over to Seton.

Leading the limping horse out of the barn, Stillman turned to the liveryman. "Anyone been messing with my horse?"

"What's wrong with your horse?"

"Got a cracked shoe."

The man's piqued gaze wilted. After a ponderous moment, he said without inflection, "I never saw nobody messin' with your horse," and went back to his work.

Stillman turned his gaze to the jailhouse beyond the paddock. Corey was sitting on the stoop, leaning back in a chair, boots propped on the hitch rack. He lifted his hat to Stillman and grinned.

Stillman stared at him, burning. Corey had cracked the shoe. Stillman would have bet his eyeteeth on that. It appeared the Lone Pine marshal was trying to put a burr under Stillman's blanket, but he had another think coming if he thought Stillman would reconsider his ride out to where Boomhauer had been killed.

The Hill County sheriff turned to the liveryman. "You do shoe work?"

"Nope. Try the blacksmith."

"Where?"

The liveryman pointed west. Stillman turned and led the horse past several shop owners sweeping their board-walks. The barber, Marv Tattersall, nodded at him cordially. Stillman found the blacksmith shop among shanties ad privies and trash heaps, several buggies and wagons parked in its yard, piles of scrap iron abutting both sides.

It was a long, low building with a tin roof, and its large doors were propped wide with barrels. The smithy was working inside, reshaping a bent wheel rim on an anvil. Fetid black smoke rose from the chimney and flattened across the roof, gritty with cinders. A small spotted pup was tied to a wagon wheel propped against the right door. It yipped at Stillman, wagging its tail and bouncing on its hind legs, wanting attention.

"Sandy, hush," the blacksmith said, stopping his hammer in mid-swing when he saw Stillman approaching with his horse.

"What can I help you with?" he asked Stillman.

"Horse has a cracked rear shoe. The right one. Can you fix me up? I'm in a hurry."

"Everyone's in a hurry," the man said in a slight Old-World accent, turning away from the anvil.

Carrying the hammer in his big right hand, he walked from the shade into the golden morning sunlight—a tall, shaggy-haired man in a leather apron and threadbare breeches from which the color had been washed long ago. His well-muscled arms were sweat-glossed and cinder-streaked.

"You that sheriff been nosin' around, eh?" Unexpectedly, the blacksmith grinned.

"That's me."

"Well, I reckon you are in a hurry then." The blacksmith chuckled and extended his hand. "Arvin Lowdermilk."

"Ben Stillman."

"Used to read about you in the papers. That's when I was still in Billings."

"How long you been here?"

"Two years." Lowdermilk shook his big, hairy head. The points of his cheekbones were pink, having been sunburned and peeled, then burned again. The rest of his face and his neck had the texture of his worn, leather apron. He smelled of hot iron and sweat.

"That Charlie Boomhauer—I liked him. We hunted birds together." He gestured at the pup, who sat eyeing Stillman, engrossed. "With that one's ma—a good springer. She's old now. I keep her up at the house."

"He's next in line, eh?" Stillman asked, kneeling down and taking the floppy-eared dog onto his knee. The pup licked his face.

Lowdermilk led Sweets to the post before the open doors and tied him. Walking around the wary-eyed bay, he lifted his hoof to inspect the shoe.

"She's cracked, all right."

"You got time?'

With a dubious smile that put Stillman a little on edge, the man returned to the dense shadows of the smelly shop and pumped the bellows.

"Any idea who killed Charlie?" Stillman asked, patting the energetic little dog, who sat up on his knee to nibble Stillman's ear.

Lowdermilk pumped the bellows and shook his head once.

While the blacksmith worked on the shoe, Stillman rolled a smoke, then sat on a barrel. He smoked and patted the pup while he watched the town coming to life. Three girls in gaudy dresses—pleasure girls from a brothel, no doubt—walked up the avenue carrying wicker shopping baskets. They smiled as they passed, and Stillman tipped his hat.

"Hi, Sandy," one of them said to the pup who watched them expectantly, ears raised.

When the man was fitting the shoe to Sweets' hoof, Stillman watched a buggy heading in his direction from

Crawford Street. It was the red-wheeled buggy from last night, and the bespectacled man in the bowler hat was driving and smoking a cigar. The same girl sat next to him. At least it looked like the same girl. She was dressed in a white dress with ruffles and fancy stitchwork on the sleeves. Her auburn hair was pulled back in a tight bun. Her face was pale and pinched.

Stillman was standing near the blacksmith.

"Hey," he said to the man. "Who's that?"

Lowdermilk turned and glanced at the buggy passing before them, the thin wheels clicking over stones. He turned quickly back to the shoe and gave a nail a tap with the hammer. "That," he said wryly, "is the banker and his lovely princess."

Lowdermilk chuckled and gave the nail another tap.

Watching the buggy disappear down the street, Stillman said, "Last night I saw them whipping through town to the doctor's office."

"No doubt."

"The girl isn't well?"

"You might say that."

Annoyed, Stillman turned to the blacksmith. "That a secret too?"

"I'll say it is." Lowdermilk was tapping again with the hammer. He stopped suddenly and straightened. Ambling heavy-heeled over to Stillman, he stopped, sleeved sweat from his forehead, and said softly, "She...uh...got herself in the family way. By the wrong boy."

"Oh."

"Kind of a family secret, you see. Kind of a town secret, too. That is, everyone knows about it, but nobody talks about it. Openly."

"Quite the scandal, I guess."

Lowdermilk guffawed, caught himself, sobered, and turned back to the horse.

When he'd finished the job, he straightened with a sigh and held out his hand. "That'll be seventy-five cents."

Stillman paid the man and mounted his horse. "Much obliged," he said.

Lowdermilk didn't say anything. He was already back at his forge, working with solemn gravity, like a chastised child.

Puzzled, Stillman studied him. Then he turned Sweets northward and rode away.

————

THE BLACKSMITH WAS SHAPING another wheel rim when the puppy yipped. Lowdermilk turned to look out the open doors, and his stomach tensed when he saw Nick Corey turn off the lane and approach the shop with that easy swagger of his and that lazy smile.

The puppy pulled at the end of its rope, hopping on its back legs and whining for attention.

Corey stopped in the sunlit yard, grinning. With an idiot's wave, he said, "Hidy, Arvin!"

By the set of the marshal's jaw, the loony cast in his eyes, and the exaggeratedly clownish smile, Lowdermilk knew there was trouble.

Cautiously studying Corey, Lowdermilk asked, "What can I do for you today, Nick?"

Corey laughed—it was more of a clipped cackle. Poking the brim of his shabby hat back on his head, he cocked a hip and said, "Well, for one thing, Arvin, you can start callin' me Marshal. I am the marshal around here now, you know."

"I reckon I know that. Reckon I know good ole Charlie was murdered by some cold-blooded devil. Shot in the back."

Corey's smile lost its luster. "Yeah, that was a tragedy it was. But tragedy or not it still leaves me the marshal—less'n of course, Mr. Drake and the rest of the town council wants to appoint someone else. I don't think they will, though. Ain't many men with my experience around here. So I'm the marshal, all right. And I'd appreciate it if you'd start using my official title."

The smile returned in full blossom. "I really would appreciate it. Otherwise, it sounds... well, it sounds disrespectful."

Lowdermilk didn't say anything. The puppy pranced on its hind legs, begging for Corey's attention.

"Sandy, lay down," Lowdermilk ordered.

"Well, look at him," Corey said, grinning at the dog. "I swear that pup grows an inch a day!"

Corey walked over to the dog, crouched down, and picked it up. The pup nibbled his ear, and he laughed. "Hey, that tickles!"

Lowdermilk watched darkly as the marshal petted his dog.

"Sure a nice little pup you have here, Arvin," Corey said. He looked at the blacksmith, his brow furrowing as though a thought had just occurred to him. "Say, that Clantick sheriff been by here? What's his name? Stiles.... Stiller... St—?"

"Stillman."

"That's right—Stillman. He been by here?"

"Yeah, he was by here. Needed a new shoe for his horse."

"You don't say," Corey said. His hands moved brusquely down the pup's wiggling body. "I bet he was full o' questions, wasn't he?"

Lowdermilk watched the deputy's hands move heavily over the pup. "He had a few."

"Curious fella, ain't he?" Corey scratched behind the pup's right ear.

Lowdermilk watched the dog and didn't say anything.

"Yeah, he sure is curious," Corey said, "for a sheriff that doesn't have no jurisdiction out here. Downright snoopy, in fact. Snoopin' into matters mat don't concern him. Pushin' his weight around."

Cory gazed at the dog. His eyes were two black coals set deep within his skull. His brows were ridged. "This pup sure has some delicate bones, don't he? Very fragile. Real fine."

"Please, don't—"

Running his large hands down the pup's neck, Cory continued. "I know how you like to talk, Arvin. But we'd just as soon you saved the chatter for the saloons, Mr. Drake and me. And even then, we both hope you won't talk about nothin' that don't concern you. 'Cause we both know how you like to watch and listen. We both know how you tend to be a little curious your ownself—stick your nose in, just like Stillman, where it don't belong."

Corey pinched the pup's ear, and it yelped. Lowdermilk jumped.

"And we—Mr. Drake and me—just wanted to let you know we know how you are, and if anything embarrassing —you know, anything no one else needs to know about— slips into the wrong pair of ears"—Corey pinched the pup's other ear, and the pup yelped and whimpered— "why we know who to talk to about it."

Corey paused, his eyes flat as a snake's as he studied the blacksmith without expression.

"You know what I'm sayin', Arvin?"

The blacksmith looked at the pup struggling in the marshal's arms. Then he looked at Corey. He swallowed, his big Adam's apple bobbing. "I hear you."

"All right then," Corey said, the smile returning to his face.

He lifted the pup, turning it in his hands, and touched the struggling pup's nose to his. "You're just the cutest thing I ever saw! You sure are, you know that!" Corey laughed and set the pup gently on the ground, and watched it slink around behind the barrel, whimpering, its tail between its legs.

"I declare—he grows an inch a day!"

Corey turned and, shoving his hands knuckle-deep in his pockets, stepped out into the lane, heading for Crawford Street

"Be seein' ye, Arvin!"

Chapter Eight

COREY'S MAP WAS EASY ENOUGH TO FOLLOW. Whether or not it was leading him anywhere, Stillman didn't know. What he did know was that he wasn't being trailed, because he'd held up for half an hour in a gully with his Henry out and ready for action, and no one had shown up.

Not even a dust plume in the distance toward town.

He'd mounted up and ridden another fifteen minutes when he paused to study the map. Gazing around at the grassy meadows and rocky ridges, which reminded him of the Two Bears south of Clantick—his home country— he found the landmark he was looking for.

Kneeing Sweets left, he crossed a low saddle, descended through aspen and then followed a creek through a park painted purple and pink by wildflowers. When he came to a fork in the horse trail, he followed the left tine over another, higher ridge.

Descending the other side, he saw a small, abandoned ranchstead in the valley below. It had to be the place Corey had drawn near the X on the map, which meant, if Corey wasn't just leading Stillman on a wild-goose chase, south-east of the ranch, about a hundred yards beyond that knoll yonder, was where Corey had discovered Boomhauer's body.

When Stillman reached the valley floor, he spurred Sweets into a canter, on a course that would take him past the cabin. He was fifty yards from the cabin when he suddenly reined the bay to a halt and quickly slid his Colt from its holster.

Before him, four horsemen rode out from behind the cabin, two on each side. They wore bags over their faces with the eyes and mouths cut out. Otherwise, they were dressed like drovers, in denims, cotton shirts, and Western hats. They wore tied-down revolvers—slick-looking guns in tricky holsters. They carried Winchesters across the pommels of their saddles.

"Don't try anything stupid, mister," one of them said. "Look behind you."

Stillman did. Three more masked riders rode out from the trees and brush along the base of the ridge. They too held Winchesters over their saddles as they approached.

Stillman turned back around. "Well, don't I look stupid," he said, holstering the .44. "I didn't know we were all supposed to wear masks to this dance."

"You're trespassin' on private property," said the man who'd spoken before—a tall hombre in a black hat with a conch-studded band. Wearing a blue shirt under a black vest, he rode a gray Arabian with a Mexican saddle and a wild look in its eye.

Stillman's bay snorted and shook its head, not liking these masked strangers a bit.

Holding his reins taut, Stillman asked with a rueful smile, "Why did I have a feeling you were going to say that? I suppose you have a rustling problem too."

"That's right," said the man on the Arab.

Stillman rubbed his jaw. "All right—I'm trespassing where rustlings occurred. I can see where that would make me a suspicious hombre. But why the masks? How do those play into your game?" He knew showing them his badge wouldn't do any good; they knew who he was.

There was a silence. Only the sounds of the horses made any noise. Fidgety, Sweets shook his head, his bridle bit bouncing in his mouth. The masked riders stared at Stillman from behind their feed sacks.

The leader said, "When we're through with you, Stillman, you're gonna want to get out of here and stay out of here. We're gonna be nice and gentle with you—this time. Next time, we won't be near so sweet."

The man nodded to someone behind Stillman. Hearing the rope, Stillman ducked, but the wide loop settled over his head and shoulders. Quickly, the slack was taken up, and Stillman was jerked out of his saddle, hitting the ground hard on his side, a sharp pain shooting through his left hip, numbing his leg.

Sweets whinnied and bucked and galloped away, kicking.

Stillman climbed to his knees and looked around, the rope pinning his arms to his sides. The riders were casually dismounting, eyes grinning, one man accepting the other men's reins. The man who had the other end of Stillman's rope sat his horse, keeping the noose so taut it was hard for Stillman to breathe.

Aflame with anger, Stillman bolted to his feet and gave the rope a mighty jerk. Caught off guard, the man holding the other end gave a startled cry and flew out of his saddle, hitting the dust face-first.

Lifting the noose above his head, Stillman tossed it aside, took two long strides to the man in the dust and swung his leg back and up, bringing the toe of his boot hard against the man's chin, flinging him over backward.

'That son of a *buck!*" someone whooped behind Stillman, as though at a friendly rodeo brawl.

Stillman turned to see the man coming at him swinging a haymaker. Stillman ducked under the punch, came up, jabbed the man twice in the gut, then lifted his knee to meet the man's face as his head plunged groundward. Stillman's knee came away wet with blood from the man's busted nose.

Another rider plunged in from Stillman's right. Stillman ducked under that blow too, and came up with a hard left, catching the man high on his cheekbone. It knocked the man backward but not down, and as the man recovered and came back for more, Stillman backed up a step, getting ready.

Something buckled his knees from behind, and he fell over the back of the man who'd gotten down on all fours behind him—the old schoolyard trick.

The man laughed as Stillman whipped to his feet, balling his fists. They were all around him now—all seven of them, two with blood on their masks. Their eyes were smiling, and they were whooping and yelling, encouraging each other.

"Okay, Gris—it's your turn, boy!" one of them yelled, shoving a slender man toward Stillman. "Let him have it!"

The slender rider swung his right first. Stillman blocked it with his forearm and gave him two staccato jabs high in the face. In the meantime, another man bolted in from Stillman's left and landed a roundhouse to Stillman's forehead, staggering him. Another one punched him twice in the face, numbing his cheek and tearing the corner of his right eye.

The lawman didn't go down, however. He faded just in

time to miss a left jab. He hadn't gotten resettled before someone kicked him in the back of his right knee. As that knee buckled, another man punched him in the jaw.

The blow threw him sideways. In one quick motion, he pushed himself off the ground with both hands and bulled into one of the masked gunmen, knocking him flat. Turning, he ducked a blow and buried his fist in a belly.

He was turning to another man when yet another punched him in the gut He was going down when a knee met his mouth, smashing his lips against his teeth, ringing his ears and starting a blaze behind his eyelids.

He was on his knees then, head thrown back, brain on fire, blood streaming from the cuts on his face. The masked men circled him slowly, cautiously, as though approaching a wounded lion in the grass.

"That son of a buck don't give up, does he?" someone asked.

"Ornery. Just plain ornery."

"Pull him up, Louis," said another. "Hold him tight."

Stillman's arms were wrenched painfully behind him. He was jerked off his knees and held there, sagging, knees wanting to buckle. His shoulders felt ready to pop from their sockets. His eyelids were too heavy and swollen to open, so he didn't see the masked gunmen close on him, but he felt the blows—one after another—to his face, belly, and groin.

He felt the first few, that is... and then everything went black.

————

TWELVE-YEAR-OLD ROBBIE TOBIAS watched the fight from the top of the hill south of the ranchstead. Robbie's horse was tethered in the trees behind and below him, the brace of quail the boy had shot earlier draped over the saddle horn.

Robbie had heard the commotion a few minutes ago, when he'd been riding on the other side of the hill, looking for more birds for his ma's stew pot. He'd reined the horse to a halt, dismounted, and climbed the hill. Kneeling down, he saw the seven masked riders fighting with the lone, unmasked man in the blue-checked shirt—a big, lean man with broad shoulders and a brushy mustache and wavy, gray-flecked hair spilling onto his collar.

You really couldn't call it a fight Not when there were seven men against one. The lone man held his own for a couple minutes, but then the seven closed on him and, while two held his arms, they beat the holy tar out of him.

Robbie watched, awestruck and elated to have come upon such a sight—he'd never seen a real fight before. Or a beating, he should say. But he was also a little fearful. What if the men in masks saw him up here? It was pretty obvious by the way they were beating the lone man, and by their laughter that they were bad. Badmen, just like in the dime stories, no doubt.

Probably Snaketrack men, for this was the outer limits of Snaketrack range. You didn't find much worse in the way of badmen around here.

Robbie's heart thumped. He wanted to get on his horse and ride away, but an awful fascination held him there.

Finally, the masked men gave the lone man their final blows and released him. He dropped face down in the dust.

He did not move as the masked men stood around him for a while, talking. They lifted their hats and removed their masks, then donned their hats again. It was too far away for Robbie to see their faces, but he could tell by the way they carried themselves, and by their well-heeled cow ponies tied near the cabin, that they were indeed "Craw-ford's firebrands," as his ma and uncle called them.

When the Snaketrack men had mounted their horses and ridden over the ridge southeast of the cabin, their dust sifting above the sage and brome, Robbie gazed down at the ranchstead. The lone man lay where the others had left him, face down in the yard.

Robbie turned and looked down the hill at his horse—a paint pony he called Injun. He considered mounting up and hightailing it away from there, pretending he hadn't seen a tiling. But his curiosity got the better of him, and when he'd walked back down to his horse and mounted up, he reined the horse along the ridge to the wagon trail.

Then he followed the trail over the ridge and into the ranch yard.

He tied Injun to the hitching post near the cabin, and then he crept cautiously over to the man who lay uncon-scious in the dust. The man's shaggy brown hair was coated with seeds and dust as was the rest of him. His face was cut and bruised, and the blood had been smeared by the fists of the Snaketrack men.

Robbie wondered if the man was alive. He knelt down a couple feet away. For some reason, he didn't want to get too close to the man. Turning an ear to listen, he heard the man's raspy breath and saw the dust puff slightly beneath his nose, where blood darkened the dirt

"Mister?" the boy asked. "You all right, there, mister?"

The man groaned.

Realizing now that the man was too injured to be dangerous, Robbie put his hand on the man's shoulder. The man groaned again, gave a start, and rolled onto his back, grimacing. He tried lifting his head, but gave up and lay back in the dirt, appearing to pass out again.

Robbie saw something poking out of the man's shirt

pocket. It was shiny and had points, like a star. Robbie glanced at the man's inert face, then back at the metal object poking out of the pocket. Hesitantly, he slid the object from the shirt and saw that it was, sure enough, a star!

Holding it up, Robbie saw the words "Hill County Sheriff."

Oh, boy! This fella's a lawman!

Clutching the star in his hand, Robbie studied the man —the Hill County sheriff—and wondered what to do. Finally deciding, he got up, ran to his horse, mounted up, and rode off at a gallop through a crease in the eastern hills.

Behind him, Stillman lifted his head again. It weighed a ton and screamed with pain. Muttering a curse, he dropped his head and passed out.

Chapter Nine

A HALF HOUR LATER, STILLMAN HEARD THE LOUD clatter of a wagon moving toward him, and he reached for the gun on his hip, but it wasn't there. Only the holster was there, its hammer thong hanging loose.

Must have fallen out during the fandango.

He looked toward the din and saw the wagon approach behind two mules. Between his swollen eyelids, he saw a man and a woman in the driver's seat, and a boy in the box.

Then he remembered a boy's voice asking him if he was all right. The voice had come from down a long tunnel, but he realized now it had not been a dream. The boy had gone for help.

Feeling queasy, Stillman closed his eyes and lay back. His head throbbed, and his stomach ached. He remembered the fists connecting with his face and gut, the grinning look in the eyes behind his attackers' masks.

He winced at the sharp pain in his lower chest. Broken ribs. In spite of his injuries, a cold fire burned in his belly, making everything very simple and clear and inevitable.

They'd wanted to frighten him off. Well, he wasn't frightened. He was more curious now than ever about Boomhauer's murder. Besides that, he was mad. Fighting mad.

And he was staying right here till he got to the bottom of the mystery.

"Robbie, fetch the canteen, will you?"

It was a woman's voice. Stillman opened his eyes to see her kneel beside him, looking with concern into his battered face. She was lovely, in her late twenties, early thirties. Oval face, clear brown eyes, thick tawny hair piled in a loose coronet. She wore a green plaid dress buttoned to the neck, with a white collar. Plain as it was, it did little to conceal her high-bosomed figure.

"You're alive," she said.

He'd lifted his head slightly, peering up at her through slitted lids.

"Rest easy," she said.

A man stood beside her, stooped over to stare down at Stillman, hands on his thighs. He was a slight man, prematurely old, with gray hair and a gray handlebar mustache browned from chew. He wore bibfront coveralls over a red plaid shirt and a frayed straw hat.

When the boy brought the canteen, the woman uncorked it, lifted Stillman's head in her right arm, and brought the canteen to his lips with her left hand. He drank a few swallows, tasting blood mixing with the water.

When she lowered the canteen, he said, "Obliged," in a tight, raspy voice.

"How bad are you hurt? Can we move you?" the woman asked.

"Just a few lumps here and there," Stillman said, pushing himself up with his hands. "I've been through worse."

He grimaced and lay back with a sigh. "The ribs seem to be grievin' me, though."

"Limon, take an arm," the woman said.

Stillman must have passed out then because he was only vaguely aware of being moved to the wagon. The wagon bounced interminably beneath him, grieving his ribs before it finally stopped. The next thing he knew he was in a small, neat bedroom with handwoven rugs on the floor, a small table against the wall to his left, with wild-flowers in a glass vase and a white enamel basin with a few black spots up near its lip where the enamel had chipped away.

The sheets and patchwork quilt pulled up to his chin were crisp and clean. His clothes and gun were draped neatly over the ladder-back chair shoved up to the table, his boots arranged neatly beneath. The clothes and boots appeared to have been cleaned.

There was a bearskin on the floor and a bobcat's hide on the wall. To his right was a sashed window. The light through the crack in the flour-sack curtains was of midday quality. He could hear birds and someone hammering an anvil.

Looking around, his chest and belly feeling as though he'd been run through with a Sioux war lance, his puffed lips grieving him no end, he could not for the life of him figure out where he was. He touched his face tenderly with his fingertips, tracing the scratches and the swelling around his eyes.

And then he remembered the seven masked riders and the people who'd come for him in the wagon. He must be at those people's cabin now.

It was hard to think clearly because his bladder was bursting at the seams. Looking to his right and down, he sighed with relief when he saw a white porcelain thunder mug. It ached like hell to reach down and remove the lid, and then to roll over, fish himself out of his underwear, and get a steady stream going in the pot, but he managed. It took forever, and his bladder was relieved afterwards, but not his ribs, which felt as though they'd been ground to powder.

That was when he realized a bandage had been wrapped around his ribs so tightly that it pinched his wind.

He'd just gotten himself in order, panting, when someone knocked softly on the door.

"Come," Stillman said, half-surprised by the almost normal sound of his voice.

The door cracked, and the woman from before peered in guardedly.

"Are you awake?"

"Yes."

Her features brightened. "How do you feel?"

"Like seven men beat the stuffing out of me. How do I look?"

Her lips formed a bemused smile as she approached the bed. "Like seven men beat the stuffing out of you. But better than you looked yesterday."

"You mean I slept a whole day?"

"Pret' near. The best thing for you, too. Ready for some light?"

Easing up in the bed and resting his head and shoulders against the headboard, he nodded. She opened the curtains on both windows, flooding the room with golden sunshine.

"There. That's better."

"Much obliged... for everything."

"My son Robbie found you. He was hunting when he heard the commotion."

"I'll thank him personally."

"He doesn't expect any thanks, Sheriff. Nor do I or Limon."

"You must have found my badge."

Standing over him, hands crossed before her again, she nodded and gestured at the table behind her. "Robbie did. It's there, with your gun. Your horse is in the corral." She smiled. "He followed you here."

"Sweets is a loyal horse."

"You must be a kind master."

Stillman studied her, impassively admiring her beauty. Her face was fine-boned and smooth, yet there was humor in her full mouth and a friendly curiosity in her brown-eyed gaze. She wore an orange flowered dress with an apron. Her tawny hair was piled atop her head, in a coronet, as when he'd first seen her.

"And you are...?"

She blushed. "Oh, where are my manners? I'm Nell. Nell Tobias."

Stillman extended his hand, wincing at the pain in his ribs. "Ben Stillman. Pleased to meet you, Mrs. Tobias. I apologize for the trouble and do not plan to bother you and your husband much longer. As soon as I can ride, I will."

She shook her head. "Limon isn't my husband. He's my brother-in-law. My husband, Roger, died two years ago.

Stillman nodded. "I'm sorry to hear that."

Her eyes dropped, and she flushed again. There was a slight pause. Then: "Are you hungry?"

"Bottomed out," Stillman said. "But please don't trouble yourself..."

"No trouble at all, Mr. Stillman. I have stew simmering on the range. Coffee?"

In spite of his split lip, Stillman smiled. "I'd give my last horse and my right arm for a cup."

"Coming right up," Nell Tobias said. She picked up his thunder mug and headed for the door.

She returned a few minutes later with stew and coffee. She went out and came back with his empty thunder mug and set it beside the bed. As he forked the stew into his mouth—succulent chunks of quail with potatoes, onions, and carrots—he noticed her studying him.

Was it curiosity or wariness in her eyes—or both? Whatever it was, she appeared troubled.

She retreated shyly from his gaze, turning and heading for the door.

Stillman swallowed and cleared his throat. "I suppose you're wondering what I'm doing in this neck of the woods and who the men were who jumped me."

She turned to face him, nervously smoothing her dress and apron against her thighs. "I think I... I think I know the answer to both of those questions," she said haltingly.

Stillman froze, watching her. She suddenly appeared nervous. "Oh?" he asked.

"When you're well enough," she said, meeting his gaze, "you best go on back to Clantick. Don't come back here."

"Don't tell me you're trying to get rid of me, too!"

"It's for your own good."

"Why don't you let me be the judge of what's good for me?" Stillman watched her standing in the doorway, smoothing the dress over her thighs. His swollen eyes puckered skeptically, and he asked with an interrogative air, "Why do you think I'm here?"

She sighed, looked at the chair where his clothes had been piled. Her features dark, she closed the door, moved to the chair, pulled it out from the table, and sat down.

Her brown eyes, round and large, met Stillman's for several seconds before she said, "It was the Snaketrack men who attacked you. They attacked you because they knew you were here investigating Charlie Boomhauer's murder. Isn't that right? Aren't you trying to figure out who killed Charlie? Charlie and the Gypsies?"

Stillman looked at her sharply. "The Gypsies are dead, too? The Gypsies that were camped out here?"

She did not respond, just watched him, as though deciding what to do. Outside, birds wheeled past the windows, and a man called for Robbie.

No longer hungry, Stillman set his stew bowl beside his coffee cup. Tell me what you know, Mrs. Tobias," he said. "Please."

She sat in silence for a long time. Finally, she swallowed.

"Lord help me," she whispered, placing her elbows on her knees and taking her face in her hands, "if I get another man killed..."

Chapter Ten

ON A BRIGHT MORNING TWO WEEKS AGO, NELL TOBIAS
had retrieved eggs from the chicken coop and was taking
them back to the cabin in a wicker basket looped around
her arm.

"Ma, look!"

She turned to her right and saw Limon and Robbie
standing in the yard before the barn, where they'd stopped
on their way to the house for breakfast. Robbie's right arm
was extended, his finger pointing east

Nell looked to the eastern hills still in morning shadows. That was when she saw the riders galloping over a
grassy ridge. There were at least a half dozen of them, and
they quickly disappeared, riding in a loose line behind a
hill.

"Snaketrack men," Limon said darkly, staring after
them.

"They seem to be in an awful hurry this morning," Nell
said. "Where do you think they're headed?"

Limon only shrugged, hooked his thumbs around his
suspenders, and continued walking toward the house.

Nell stared eastward for several more seconds, feeling vaguely
apprehensive about the riders. She'd known from experience the Snaketrack riders were trouble, for Max Crawford had tried to root her and her late husband, Roger, and Limon and Robbie out of this valley, which he wanted for his expanding cattle herd.

"Everything's all right—ain't it, Ma?" Robbie asked. "They won't bother us, will they?"

Nell looked down at her young son. She forced a smile, placed her hand on the back of his neck, giving a reassuring squeeze, and said, "Everything's fine, Robbie. Now go wash for breakfast."

The boy nodded and jogged to the house, and Nell followed him, casting her glance once more to the east.

She'd nearly put the riders out of her mind when, twenty minutes later, during breakfast, she heard the gunfire. She froze with a forkful of eggs halfway to her mouth and turned to the normally placid Limon—poor, simple Limon, who'd never married and who'd been cared for all his life by his older brother, Roger until Roger died.

Limon looked at her fearfully, the upswept ends of his gray mustache twitching. Robbie was looking at her too.

The boy was first to speak. "Those are gunshots, Ma."

Nell scraped her chair back and walked to the door, peering southwest. She stood there over a minute, hearing the gunfire—sporadic shots from deep in the hills. They sounded like firecrackers—only they were not what pistols and rifles sounded like even from a distance.

They came from the general direction of where the Gypsies were camped.

Finally, Limon cleared his throat. "They're... they're prob'ly just tryin' to pop calves and their mommas out of the brush back in them cuts."

Finally, the gunshots tapered and then ceased. Her heart thumping in her chest and a dull ringing in her ears, Nell said, "Yes. That must be what they're doing."

But she thought about the gunfire all the rest of the day and evening, and for several hours before she finally slept that night. After breakfast the next morning, she asked, "Robbie, saddle Donner for me, will you?"

"Where you going, Ma?"

"Just saddle him please, Robbie."

"Yes, ma'am," the boy said, rising from his chair and brushing past Nell as he left the cabin, heading for the corral.

Nell went into her bedroom and changed into riding slacks. Coming out, she strapped a wide-brimmed straw hat to her head. Limon was still at the table, his back stiff, face grim.

"I'll check on them for you, Nell," he said halfheartedly, having read her concern.

"No, you stay here with Robbie, Limon," Nell said, moving quickly through the door.

Robbie had the white-stockinged black saddled and waiting outside the corral. Nell climbed into the saddle with the ease and sureness of a woman nearly as accustomed to riding as a man, and said, "Thank you, Robbie. You know your chores for the morning, don't you?"

"Yes, ma'am."

"Mind Limon. I'll be back soon."

With that, she reined the horse around and heeled him westward, following the wagon trail, then cutting through Bear Hollow to Bear Creek, which she followed for a mile, rising steadily through the hills where the grass grew deep, and the wildflowers splashed the meadows with all the colors of the rainbow. When she came to the meadow where the Gypsies had parked their wagons and erected their tents, she halted the black horse suddenly and stared.

The meadow was empty. No wagons or tents or cook-fires. No Gypsies with their colorful clothes and their bois-terous laughter. No laundry boiling in tubs or gutted deer carcasses hanging from trees.

Toeing the horse ahead through the torn, trampled grass, she came to a ravine. There were many hoofprints along the rim, and the bank had been caved in. Over the mound of clay and dirt at the bottom, rocks had been heaped.

A grave.

Nell's heartbeat fiercely, as though pumped by a giant's fist Tears of fear and outrage sprang to her eyes. Seeing something wink in the grass nearby, she heeled the horse over to it, looking down. In the matted green grass, beside a torn and trampled pink flower, lay a brass shell casing.

Nell scrambled down from her horse and dropped to her knees, retching and crying. She felt as though her stomach had been pumped full of kerosene. When she was through retching, she remained on her knees and sobbed, turning her watery gaze around the meadow that had become, she knew, a killing ground.

Finally, she mounted her horse and galloped back the way she had come. But when she got to the wagon road, she turned south instead of east. She rode hard all the way to town, and she found Charlie Boomhauer walking back from his house after lunch, a newspaper clamped under his arm, a toothpick in his mouth.

When he finally got Nell settled down enough to tell him what had gotten her so upset, he stared at her skepti-cally, his kind blue eyes twinkling, sucking his bottom lip.

"Well, I just don't see how that coulda happened, Mrs.

Tobias," he said, glancing off with consternation. "I mean, who would want to kill those harmless folks?"

"I just told you what I saw, Sheriff," Nell said, dabbing at her puffy eyes with a handkerchief.

Boomhauer nodded. "Well, I reckon I better ride out and check it out."

"A few hours later, he was dead," Nell said. "One of those varmints from the Snaketrack shot him."

"How do you know?" Stillman asked her.

"Of course, they killed him because they didn't want him investigating the murder of the Gypsies. They probably would have killed me too, if they'd known I'd heard their gunfire and told Charlie... poor Charlie." Her voice broke, and she bowed her head with a sob.

"How does Corey fit in?" Stillman asked.

She looked at him, her eyes bright with tears. "He rode out and found the body."

"Are you sure he rode out later? He didn't leave town with Boomhauer?"

Nell shrugged. "I... I guess I don't know. That's what he said—that he rode out later when Charlie hadn't come back and found him in the meadow." She gazed at Stillman wonderingly. "Why don't you believe him?"

"Well, for one thing, he directed me out here to that Snaketrack committee."

"He used to ride for Crawford."

"He did?"

"Sure," Nell said. "That's how he got the deputy marshal's job. Crawford and Drake are business partners."

Stillman was frowning. "Wait, wait. Who's Drake?"

"The only banker in town."

"Banker," Stillman said, pondering, remembering his conversation with the blacksmith.

"He's also president of the town council. Has a hand in

everything, including the marshal's office. Charlie was always griping about him, how he's always playing God with the whole county."

"Drake plays God with the whole county, eh? That means he probably jerks Corey's strings too—especially since Drake and Crawford were the ones who got Corey the badge in the first place."

"Do you think Drake was involved in the murder of the Gypsies?"

"I don't know, but I bet he had a hand in Boomhauer's. He would have known if Corey intended to kill the town marshal since he's the head man in Lone Pine. He would have at least had to clear it if he didn't order it. And covering up the killing of the Gypsies would be in his own best interests since he and Crawford are partners."

Stillman shook his head, lifted his arms, and dropped them helplessly. "But I'm just speculating. I don't know what to think. I am getting one hell of a headache, and I don't think it's just because my head's been busted, either."

"I'll let you sleep," Nell said, rising from her chair.

"Wait," Stillman said urgently. "I need to know where the Gypsies and Boomhauer were killed. Was it near the place the Snaketrack men jumped me?"

Nell shook her head. "It's nowhere near there. It's south and west of here, about a mile and a half as the crow flies."

"Will you show me?" Excited, Stillman tossed his covers back.

"Now? Good heavens, you need rest!"

"I need to see that meadow more than I need rest," the sheriff said.

But when he'd dropped his feet to the floor, he froze with a sigh, wincing as his ribs squealed in misery.

"On second thought," he rasped through a taut sigh,

gently lowering himself back onto his elbows, "I guess it can wait till tomorrow."

When she'd helped Stillman back into bed, fluffing his pillow and pulling his covers up to his chest, Nell quietly left the room with his bowl and coffee cup. As she closed the door behind her, she became aware of her reluctance to leave his side.

Bruised and battered as he was, his presence made her feel safe, and she hadn't felt truly safe, with Crawford's men near, for a long time. More man that, Stillman was an attractive man with a warm light in his eyes, and a large spirit A good man. A man like her Roger had been.

A man who made her feel like a woman.

How long had it been since she'd been with a man? Over two years now... nearly three...

Chapter Eleven

STILLMAN MADE HIMSELF SLEEP FOR THE REST OF the day—not an easy task for a man with a lot on his mind. But he knew it was the only way he'd heal enough to get moving again tomorrow.

He slept later than he'd expected the next morning, and by the time he'd dressed and left the bedroom, Nell Tobias, her son, and her brother-in-law were seated at the breakfast table. Robbie and Limon had cloth bibs tucked into their shirts.

"Good morning, Sheriff," Nell said with a pretty smile. "How do you feel, sir?"

"Thanks to your strap around my ribs, I don't feel half bad."

"I could have served you in bed. I don't mind."

Stillman shook his head. "Not necessary. I'm fit and ready, if you are, to take a look at... well, you know," he said, seating himself stiffly in the chair on the other end of the table from Limon, who watched him bashfully, as did the boy.

"Yes," Nell said with a visible shudder. "I've no desire to

ever see the place again myself, but I'll take you there since you're so determined."

She stood and busied herself at the stove, filling a plate. "I don't see how it's going to do any good, though. I mean, they were just Gypsies, which to most folks means they were little better than trash-heap rats. And of course, Crawford and Drake have blamed Charlie's death on rustlers. Rustlers long gone from the country."

"That may be so," Stillman said, "but if I can prove the Gypsies were indeed killed and that Boomhauer was killed when he went out to investigate their murders, I'll have a concrete reason to call in the sheriff from Chinook, and possibly federal marshals from Helena."

Nell set a plate of eggs, bacon, and buttered biscuits before Stillman. "I suppose that means you'll have to..." Her voice trailed off, and her face was pale.

"Dig into the grave," Stillman said. "I'm sorry. It's a grisly task, but you won't have a part in it—aside from getting me out there, that is. I just need hard evidence mat murder was committed."

"Why?" Nell asked dully, retaking her chair. "Why would Crawford want those poor people dead?"

"I reckon they were on his range," Stillman said, pouring coffee from the stout pot on the table. "And if they'd butchered some of his beeves..." He shook his head, scowling. "It sure didn't give him the right to do what he did—if he did it, that is—but it sure gives him a motive for murder."

'There were twelve of them," Nell said, her eyes down-cast. "Twelve lovely people. I traded with them some. Eggs for buttons and thread. Sometimes I took them buttermilk in return for pot and pan repair."

"They could shoe a horse good too," Limon said. It

was the first time he'd spoken, and Stillman looked at the man. Limon shyly averted his gaze.

"Did they ever throw any long loops?" Stillman asked him.

Nell said, "Oh, they might have butchered a cow or two. They weren't angels. But that wouldn't give Crawford cause to kill them all!"

"I'm not saying it would," Stillman said, shoveling eggs in his mouth. "But it could have set him off. He might've killed Boomhauer to keep him quiet."

"Poor Charlie," Nell said.

"It's not your fault," Stillman told her. "You reported a crime that's all." He placed his hand on hers. She lifted her eyes to his and smiled.

————

AFTER BREAKFAST, Nell had Robbie and Limon hitch a horse to a wagon; she didn't think Stillman should be riding horseback yet. Reluctantly, Stillman agreed. He'd have felt better on Sweets, but he knew that sitting a wagon would be a lot easier on his ribs.

When the rig was ready, Stillman and Nell walked together from the cabin, Stillman carrying his Henry and his canteen, his hat tipped back on his head. Nell wore fawn-colored slacks, a blue blouse with a white collar and sleeves. Over the blouse, she wore a fringed vest hand-sewn from deer hide. She wore a brown felt hat, and her tawny hair fell down her back in a braided ponytail.

Limon stood holding the horse's bridle while Robbie placed two shovels beside Stillman's rifle in the box. Turning to his mother, the boy asked, "Can I come along?"

"I should say not," Nell said sternly. "I never want you near that awful place."

"Oh, Ma."

"You heard your mother," Limon said.

Stillman went around to the right side of the wagon and saw a wood crate had been placed there as though for a step. He glanced at the boy, whose eyes watched him expectantly. Stillman smiled and nodded.

"Much obliged, son."

"I thought it'd be easier for you to have a step, Mr. Stillman. On account o' your ribs an' all."

"It would at that. Thank you."

"Oh, it weren't nothin'."

"Wasn't," Nell corrected the boy.

Using the crate, Stillman climbed into the wagon, keeping his back stiff so as not to grieve his ribs. Tipping his hat to Limon, he said, "Obliged, sir. I'll have the woman of the place back in a few hours."

The bashful man just grinned, then stepped back as Nell flicked the reins and the wagon spun out of the yard, following the trail eastward through the grassy buttes.

"Nice boy you have there, Mrs. Tobias," Stillman said as she drove, holding the reins lightly in her hands.

"Please call me Nell," she said. "Yes, I think Robbie's turned out rather well, in spite of his father dying on him. Limon's been good to him. He's a kind man, though he's never been right since the War."

"Wounded?'

'Twice in the same leg, but I think it's more what he saw that touched him. Were you involved?"

"Yes, ma'am," Stillman said, giving his head a single wag. "The Pennsylvania Volunteers."

"Roger was involved too, but he made out better than Limon. They came West together, the two brothers. Before Roger died, I don't think they were ever more man fifty feet apart." She looked at Stillman, smiling broadly, and said, "Made it a little difficult during Roger's and my honeymoon, as you might imagine." She chuckled huskily.

Stillman threw his head back with a delighted laugh. "Mrs. Tobias—Nell, I mean—your sense of humor reminds me of my lovely wife's."

"I had a feeling you were married."

"Why's that?'

Nell shrugged and stared off, pensive. "Just a feeling..."

Stillman glanced at her. He could tell by her demeanor that she felt the same attraction toward him that he felt toward her. He'd never felt anything like it since he'd met Fay and fallen in love with the beautiful French rancher's daughter. Oh, a woman or two had turned his head, but he'd never felt the pull a man can feel for a woman he feels an inner kinship with. Until now. He knew it was more than lust, and because it was, it frightened him a little.

Changing the subject, he asked, "How much farther?"

"About fifteen more minutes. We're taking the long way around, due to the wagon." Nell paused. Staring straight ahead, she asked, "What's her name?"

Stillman smiled to himself. "Fay."

"Lovely."

"It fits her."

Stillman glanced around at the grass and the hills lifting to pine-studded ridges, a pair of golden eagles circling a wooded butte to the west. Above the wagon's clatter and the horse's hooves clomping along the trail, songbirds sang, and crickets chirped. High, puffy clouds hung motionless in the baby-blue sky, which was so large it made everything on the ground look small and far away.

"Her father owned a ranch down on the Yellowstone," he said. "That's where I met her."

"How long have you been married?"

'Two years." He shook his head with disbelief. "My, how time flies."

"What made you quit marshaling?"

"Heard about that, did you?"

"Why, you're famous around here, Mr. Stillman!" She smiled delightedly.

Again, Stillman shook his head. Fame for doing his job had always amazed him, and he'd chalked it up to the newspapermen's love of colorful stories served up with a good dose of horse manure. Lawmen and desperadoes: nothing more colorful man that. While the doctor and the rancher and the gandy dancer, heroes in their own right, albeit less glamorous ones, lived and died without glory.

"I took a bullet in the back," Stillman said. "That's why I quit."

"Oh, that's right. Down in Virginia City."

Stillman nodded and lit the cigarette he'd been rolling. "To make a long story short, I nearly drank myself to death, met Fay, and decided if I was going to die, I'd just as soon do it wearing a badge as at some faro table in Great Falls. Thus the sheriff's job in Clantick."

She asked what had brought him this way, and he told her about the long-loopers he'd been tracking. By the time he'd finished, she'd halted the wagon about fifty yards from a deep ravine. The sun was warm, but the air was cooler up there. The aspen leaves rattled and flashed morning gold.

Not saying anything, Nell stared straight ahead. "This is the place," she said grimly. "In that ravine. I'd just as soon wait here if you don't mind."

Stillman took a drag off his cigarette, then climbed down from the wagon, moving deliberately and wincing when pain touched his ribs. He dropped the quirley stub, ground it out with his boot, and removed one of the shovels from the wagon box.

He swung the spade over his shoulder as he turned and started walking toward the ravine.

He studied the ground as he walked, noting the occasional shod hoof print, the torn and matted grass, and the wildflowers. In addition, mere were splashes and splatters of dried blood covered with flies, and here and there brass shell casings winked in the sun. Inspecting one of the casings, he saw it belonged to a Winchester .44—a common saddle gun.

With a dark feeling in his gut, he approached the ravine and looked down, where the lip had been caved over the side and covered with rocks. He climbed down, removed several of the heavy stones, and began digging. After a few minutes, he stopped to remove his hat and gun belt, then resumed his grim job—stabbing the spade into the mound, stabbing it deeper with the sole of his boot, lifting a shovelful of dirt and sod, and tossing it aside with a painful sigh as his ribs cried out in complaint

Something shone between two rocks to his left, and he stooped to retrieve it—a five-pointed sheriff's star, the backside tarnished with dried blood. Stillman's own blood quickened as he pocketed the star and resumed digging with fervor.

In less than fifteen minutes, he'd uncovered one hand and a bloated torso—all the evidence he needed that bodies had been buried there. He set down the shovel and walked downstream. In ten minutes, he returned, picked up the shovel, and climbed the bank. The spade on his shoulder, he walked back to the wagon, his blue eyes flinty, his jaw set in a hard line, his shirt soaked with sweat

"Well, I can call in the county sheriff now," he said darkly, climbing the wagon and taking a seat beside Nell.

She didn't say anything. She slapped the reins against the horse's back, and they started off.

At length, she asked, "What about their wagons, their stock?"

"I found the wagons downstream, just around the bend from the grave. They'd been set on fire, but they didn't burn all the way. The stock was probably scattered."

Stillman mopped the sweat from his face with a hand-kerchief and began rolling a cigarette to rid his nose of the death smell.

"Why?" Nell asked softly.

"I don't know," Stillman replied, licking the rolling paper, "but I'm going to find out."

As if to punctuate the sentence, a distant rifle popped, and a bullet tore through the wagon's end board with a splintering bark.

Chapter Twelve

STILLMAN WHIPPED HIS head around. Four horsemen thundered toward him and Nell, triggering pistols and rifles, hat brims wind-blasted against their foreheads.

"Drive!" Stillman yelled to Nell.

Ignoring the pain in his ribs, he climbed back into the box and grabbed the Henry. Settling himself against the driver's box, he jacked a shell in the chamber, raised the barrel, and drew a bead on one of the riders fifty yards behind and quickly closing. He fired, the rifle jumping in his arms. He missed his target, but he'd come close enough to give the gunmen pause. They drew back on their reins and ducked. Two squeezed off pistol shots, and Stillman replied with another blast from the Henry.

One of the horses went down face-first, its rider flying over its head. The man got up, grabbed his rifle from the saddle boot, and climbed onto the horse of the rider who'd swung back for him.

Then the four came on again, on three horses. But they moved more slowly now, cautiously spreading out in a wide arc behind the wagon, which was gaining ground as Nell yelled to the black in the traces and whipped the reins against its back.

Stillman squeezed off another round to hold the riders at bay, then swung his gaze ahead. Pointing, he yelled, "Break off through those buttes!"

"We'll never make it through!"

"I don't intend to make it through!"

Nell shot him a fearful look, then reluctantly swung the horse off the trail. The wagon bounced over stones and hummocks and caromed through shrubs. In a crease between buttes, Stillman yelled, "Rein him in."

Nell leaned back on the reins, bracing her wide-spread feet on the footboard. When the skittish black finally stopped, Stillman jumped out of the wagon. He gave Nell his Henry and the canteen they'd brought.

"Watch behind us," he told her. "You see 'em coming, squeeze off a couple rounds."

"What are you going to do?" Her face was pale, but she had her fear on a short leash.

"We'll never make it in that wagon," Stillman said, moving to the shaft.

Nell stood guard with the Henry while Stillman unhitched the horse, quickly fashioned a hackamore from the reins, and climbed aboard, wincing and sweating as his ribs protested the maneuver. He extended his hand to Nell. She gave him his rifle, took his hand, and climbed onto the horse, wrapping her arms around his waist and glancing fearfully behind.

Stillman heeled the black, yelling *"Hee-ya, horse, go!"* and they were off at a run.

A gun barked behind them, the bullet clipping an aspen branch to their right. Stillman looked behind. The four hard cases galloped past the abandoned wagon, two wielding pistols, the other two holding rifles. Their faces shone molten red around the white of their bared teeth.

"They're closing on us!" Nell yelled as another bullet whined past their heads.

"He-ya, horse, he-*yahh!*"

Stillman pushed the horse hard, turning him this way and that through buttes and hills and cuts. When he turned through shrubs into a dry creek bed, he lost the riders for several minutes. Holding the black to a plodding run, he tossed another look behind and saw the gunmen following once more, storming around a bend in the rocky arroyo, about sixty yards away.

He cursed as he felt the black slowing, heard it blowing. He and Nell rounded another bend, and he looked up the pine-studded mountain on his left. About halfway to the ridge, he saw the dark, round portal of a cave yawning in an outcropping of black volcanic rock.

Hauling back on the reins, Stillman halted the exhausted horse and swung his right leg over the black's neck, dismounting. "Come on," he told Nell, reaching up to help her down.

"What are we doing?" she cried, casting a fearful look down the creek bed, where the pursuers' horses clattered over rocks, just around the bend.

The canteen slung over his shoulder, and his rifle in his right hand, Stillman grabbed Nell's hand and pulled, nearly jerking her off her feet As he ran, he said, "Cave yonder... we're gonna make for it!"

Stillman scrambled up the side of the mountain, falling to his hands and knees as his boots slipped on the spongy turf littered with pine cones and needles and smelling of mold and pine resin. He jerked Nell along behind him, dragging her when she fell, pulling her down when he slipped. They zigzagged through the lodgepoles, climbing the steep mountain at an angle, Stillman using the tree trunks and sparse junipers to pull him along.

Gunfire sounded below. Slugs plunked into the pines.

Stillman looked up the mountain. The cave was about thirty feet away, straight above them. He swung Nell around in front of him and gave her a shove.

"Go! Head for the cave!"

Stepping behind a pine, he levered a shell in the Henry's breech. He looked down the mountain. The four men were spread out along the base of the grade, shaded by the trees, moving toward him with their faces lifted. All carried rifles now. Behind them, the creek bed shone bright with sunlight.

Stillman brought the Henry to his shoulder and planted a bead on one of the gunmen. Just before he fired, the man saw him and jumped behind a tree. Stillman's shot sailed wide. He fired twice more, hitting little but air and trees as the gunmen ducked behind pines and boulders. Then he turned and ran up the mountain.

The gunmen's rifles popped behind him, the slugs tearing up sod and pine needles at his ankles. Reaching the cave at a dead run, he ducked inside, dropped to his knees, turned, and fell to his elbows. He squeezed off three quick shots down the mountain, at the rifle barrels and hat brims and bandannas poking out from behind trees and mossy rocks.

He ducked as a sudden fusillade spat the cones and pebbles before him, and ricocheted off the shell-like rock on either side of the cave.

The shooting continued for close to a minute. Stillman weathered it by staying far enough back from the cave's entrance that the gunmen couldn't get a bead on him, and by burying his face in his arms as the cones, dirt, and pebbles pelted his hat.

When the shooting fizzled, he lifted a look over the brow of the mountain. Two of the gunmen were on the move, crouching and zigzagging behind pines. Stillman checked their ascent with three quick rounds, hearing the hot, spent cartridges fall on the rocky floor around him. He pulled his head back inside the cave when another gunman, lower down the mountain, stepped out from behind a boulder with his rifle raised.

The bullet entered the cave and spanged off a wall with an angry squeal. Stillman looked for Nell. The cave was considerably larger than its opening, and she was a good five feet behind him, shielded from the gunmen. She sat against the wall, her head buried in her upraised knees and arms, in no immediate danger of direct shots or ricochets... as long as Stillman could hold the gunmen at bay.

Fortunately, he had the high ground, and the cave, apparently a bubble in a big volcanic dike, protected his flank. Also, there was little cover for a hundred feet below the cave, as the soil was too thin for trees. The gunmen couldn't storm the cave without leaving themselves vulnerable to Stillman's Henry.

The gunmen fired again, and Stillman waited till the barrage had fizzled to begin one of his own, keeping the Snaketrack riders pinned down. When the Henry was empty, he backed up beside Nell and began thumbing shells from his cartridge belt.

Inserting them into the Henry's loading tube, he glanced at the shadows toward the cave's rear. He was pleasantly surprised to see that the cave, narrowing to a slim corridor, extended deeper into the mountain than he had originally thought. Could there be a back door?

Unable to see into the darkness, he turned to Nell.

"Do me a favor, will you?" he asked.

She looked at him, her eyes wide and fear-glazed, her

face bleached under the coating of sweat-streaked dust. She wasn't hearing him.

"Nell," he said, raising his voice, 'Take my matches and see if there's another way out of this place."

"We're going to die--"

He took her by the shoulders and shook her. "We're not going to die. I got you into this, so I'll get you out." He gave her his box of sulfur matches after removing two for himself. "Here."

She was watching him, drawing strength from him, her heart slowing, her breath moderating. She took the matches, lit one, and on her hands and knees, crawled back into the shadows.

Stillman slid the Henry's loading tube back into the stock, then crawled up to the entrance. He removed his hat and lifted a look over the lip of the mountain and down the grade, where the tall, dark pines alternated columns of golden sunlight. A gunman was waiting for him, extending his rifle and sighting down the barrel.

Stillman ducked as the gun barked, the slug spitting black chunks of rock—the same sponge-shaped stuff of which the dike was made and which lined the cave. Stillman extended his rifle to return fire, but another gunman beat him to the punch, grazing his cheek as the slug tore into the rock behind him.

Stillman retreated several feet inside the cave and thumbed the blood from his face. He knew he wasn't going to win a shootout with these men. They were dug in too well, and they were good marksmen. Not only that but they probably had five or six times more ammo. Stillman had sixteen shots in the Henry and six in his revolver, but even adding the five left in his cartridge belt, he was in a fix.

He couldn't trade any more lead unless he was certain

of a kill. About all he could do was keep them away from the cave and hope for a miracle, like a back door.

As if his thought had summoned her, Nell appeared in the shadows at the back of the cave, her face and clothes coated with charcoal-colored dust. She sat down against the wall and hung her head, giving it a single shake.

"I went... I went probably fifty feet. Nothing. Just darkness and there were bats hangin' all around in there." She gave a shudder and grabbed her shoulders.

Reclining on his right elbow, his Henry beside him, Stillman sighed. He lifted his hands and rubbed his face. The shooting had stopped. The shooters were waiting for a target.

"We'll get out of this," Stillman said, as much to himself as to Nell. He lifted another look through the opening, seeing nothing but the trees and part of a hat brim extending from behind a boulder. "We'll wait until dark, and then we'll make a run for it. I'll send you one way, and I'll go another, slinging lead to draw their fire."

"You won't make it—not against four."

"It's chancy, but I'll raise holy hob. Long enough for you to get clear, anyway. You good on your feet? Can you run?"

She stared at him, the terror in her eyes diluted by... what? A wet sheen drew over them. She didn't say anything, just looked at him that inscrutable way, her lips folded inward. He turned away, unable to bear the weight of her tenderness.

"I'm sorry, Nell," he said tiredly, turning his mind on a different track. "I'd see if they'd let you go—you being a woman an' all—but you're as dangerous to them as I am, knowing what you know."

He scowled and cursed, picking up a rock and throwing it sidearmed against the wall. "I should've suspected Crawford would have men keeping an eye on that burial site. I don't know what I was thinking, having you take me out there."

"What's done is done," she said calmly. "I don't blame you. The man to blame is Crawford." She laughed, but it was more of a grunt wrung of all humor. "My suitor!"

Stillman turned to her again, his dusty brows ridged. "You're gonna have to nail that one down for me."

"After Roger died," she explained, "Max asked me to marry him. He's expanding his ranch, and he wants my graze and water. He thought we could merge our operations. I told him no but he kept riding over to ask me, threatening me in his own subtle way. I suspect he'll try burning me out before long. Only now... I guess he won't have to..."

Time passed slowly. After a half hour, a man called from below. "Why don't you come out, Stillman? You're not goin' anywhere. You gotta be low on shells and water."

When Stillman did not reply, there came a muffled snicker.

Stillman sat against the wall opposite Nell. He built a cigarette, lit up with one of the two matches he'd taken from the box, and smoked it, keeping his eyes peeled on the opening and the clearing before the cave. Nell dozed, woke with a start, looked for Stillman, found him, and dozed again. There was something about the smoothness of her dust-streaked face, canted back against the wall as she slept, that made him want to caress it with his hand. The top buttons of her blouse had come undone, exposing just enough white lace and cleavage to prick his desire.

She was a lovely woman... but he was a married man. Married to a woman he loved more than life itself.

Outside, birds sang in the trees, and squirrels chattered. The breeze brushed the pine tops, creaking the trunks and

making an occasional soft whistle as it funneled into the
cave, swirling the pine needles and crushed cones on the
floor. Mud swallows flew in, saw the interlopers, and flew
out again, screeching angrily.

At length, the light softened as the sun fell. The sky
turned dusky, and a mourning dove cooed.

"What if one of them rides back to the ranch for more
men?" Nell asked.

Stillman turned to her, surprised that she was awake.
"How far is it—ten, twenty miles...?"

"Fifteen, at least."

"They wouldn't make it back before nightfall. Hell,
they wouldn't make it back before midnight, and these
boys would be shorthanded." Stillman shook his head.
"No, they'll stay where they are, try to take us themselves
after dark. But we'll beat 'em to the punch."

Stillman rolled another cigarette and lit it with the stub
of his old one. He stole a peek down the mountain, the
cigarette in his lips, and frowned. He saw nothing of the
men. No gun barrels or hat brims extended from behind
trees or boulders. No smoke puffs from cigarettes. He
heard none of the muffled, desultory chatter he'd heard
before.

He had a funny feeling, a prickling under his collar.
Had he been wrong about the gunmen's intentions?

Shortly, he heard low rumbling, like a distant storm.
But the sky was clear, with no clouds fleecing the blue.

Then the ground vibrated, shuddered. Stillman looked
down. The rumbling grew, like an earthquake or a train
approaching full-throttle. Nell looked around, fearfully
puzzled, saying something Stillman couldn't hear above the
roar.

Stillman was moving toward the entrance, baffled, his
blood icing when chunks of the cave's roof started raining

down on top of him. Nell cried out. There was an enormous boom, making the earth jump and shudder. Stillman looked outside to see a boulder tumble over the cave's entrance and down the mountain, churning dust, mowing shrubs, and careening off trees.

More of the ceiling caved in. Seeing that more rocks were rolling down the mountain and over the cave, Stillman grabbed Nell and pulled her deeper into the alcove's shadows, shielding them with his upraised arm and rifle, stumbling over stones. He'd pulled her about ten yards when the ceiling opened up a fissure, both sides of the fissure dropping downward.

His heart beating his ribs, Stillman knew there was nothing to do, nowhere to go, but deeper into the cave—deeper into the mountain. He'd pulled Nell several more yards into the narrowing cavity, hearing the screeching of fleeing bats and the thunder of the rock slide like warring thunderheads. Then he fell over a rock and hit the ground on his back, pulling Nell down on top of him.

A great blast of air and soot racked and engulfed him, sucking the breath from his lungs, stinging his eyes and ringing his ears, building a painful pressure in his head.

Then suddenly there was silence, like a vast held breath.

On his back, Stillman stared up at the ceiling, ears tolling, seeing nothing but stygian darkness. His nose and lungs ached from the grit in the heavy, warm air fetid with dust and sulfur.

He slid Nell aside and sat up, looking back the way they had come. There was no light where the entrance should have been, and with a feeling like lead filling his bowels, he knew why.

There was no longer an entrance to the cave.

He and Nell were entombed.

Chapter Thirteen

NELL GROANED SOFTLY. Stillman's voice boomed in the sudden, heavy silence. "Are you all right?"

"Yeah. I hit my head," she said, "but... I'm all right. My God. What happened?"

Stillman held her arm, but it was so dark that he couldn't see her.

"There must have been boulders on the mountain. Appears they rolled 'em down on top of us, crushed the cave."

Nell said nothing, but Stillman could feel the horror at work inside her. She was trying to fight it, but it fought her back hard. Stillman felt it inside himself as well—the cold, primal fear of being buried alive. Of having a whole mountain come down on top of you.

They may have been safe in the cavity for now, but soon the air would run out.

A feeble shuffling sounded to Stillman's right. It was followed by a soft screech. An injured bat, its wing probably torn.

Stillman released Nell and climbed to his feet, grunting

and sighing as his ribs cried out from behind the bandage, which had loosened. Extending his hands blindly in the darkness, he walked back toward the cave's opening and stumbled over rubble. He regained his balance and extended both hands, touching cold, hard, jagged-edged rock all the way to the ceiling.

"Crap," he said. He lit his last match. The small, buttery glow revealed only stone, and then it withered and died, and the stygian dark enfolded him once again.

"What is it?"

Stillman did not respond. Instead, he went to work moving rock, frantically removing one chunk after another. The stones were heavy, however, and some wouldn't budge from the wall. He quickly tired in the warm, heavy air, his ribs squealing for surcease. He stumbled back, felt for a stone, and slumped onto it with a sigh.

There were at least thirty square yards of rock between him and freedom, and they were locked tight for the centuries.

In the darkness, Nell sobbed.

Stillman rested, slumped forward, hands on his knees. At length, he stood and stumbled back the other way. He tripped over Nell's feet in the narrow cavity.

"Sorry," he said. "I'm going on back; see what there is to see back here... if anything."

Nell only sobbed into her hands.

The corridor was dank and as dark as the rest. There was no light anywhere, no trace of fresh air. Just the smell of mushrooms and bat guano and the occasional scuttle of a mouse or a rat. When Stillman had walked about twenty yards, he smelled and heard the faint trickle of water. Extending his hand to the left wall, he felt wet stone and sparse tufts of greasy moss.

Ten more yards and the corridor narrowed to a slit through which he could not move even sideways.

Crestfallen, he moved slowly back the way he had come, hands extended, pushing off the walls on both sides of the corridor. He knew he was back where he'd started when he heard Nell inhale raggedly.

"Anything?" she asked, her voice small and tight.

"Nothing. Where are you?"

"Here."

He felt around for her hand. Finding it, he enclosed it in his and sat down beside her, his back to the wall.

"We're socked in pretty tight, I'm afraid," he said.

She sniffed. Her shoulder moved as she sleeved tears from her face. "I guess this is it then, isn't it?"

He thought about it, trying to work his mind around the idea that they were doomed. He'd been in some pinches before, and he'd always figured a way out. His instinct was to keep moving, to keep trying... but this, he knew, was hopeless.

The thing he'd feared most—leaving Fay alone—had finally happened. He just wished it would have happened a little sooner. If he was going to die, he'd have preferred dying in the cave-in to dying here, slowly, sucking up all his oxygen till there was nothing left to suck, wracked with guilt over getting an innocent woman killed.

He held Nell's hand, caressing it with his fingers, feeling her tremble. He wrapped his arm around her shoulders, pulled her close, and kissed her forehead.

"I'm so sorry, Nell. So, so sorry..."

———

AT EIGHT O'CLOCK THAT NIGHT, Max Crawford stepped through the door of his sprawling ranch house and stood on the wide, stone veranda. A long-legged, high-waisted man with a round paunch pushing out his white silk shirt and camelhair jacket, and wearing a silver-plated six-shooter in a tooled, bull-hide holster, Crawford pulled on the riding gloves that matched his coat.

Under thick gray brows, he scrutinized the interconnecting corrals below the hill.

His drovers were in the main paddock, putting on a little rodeo to kill time before dark—all twenty of them, it appeared. The cook was at the windmill near the L-shaped bunkhouse, drawing water for dishwashing, and for the endless coffee the men always consumed while fleecing each other at cards. Beyond the ranch buildings, the gaunt hills turned brown and gold as the sun sank behind the western mesas and rimrocks.

Crawford had pulled on the second glove and was about to move off the porch, but stopped when he glimpsed movement in the east.

Turning that way, he saw four riders cantering along a hogback. They disappeared down a declivity, then lifted over another hogback, splashed across the stream, and threaded the peninsula of aspens at the edge of the ranch yard.

They mounted the hill, kicking their tired mounts into a tight-legged gallop, and headed for the house.

Crawford squinted, his brick-red face bunched with puzzlement, his thin lips drawn back from his small, square teeth. He didn't say anything as the four riders came on.

"Mr. Crawford," the lead rider said.

His name was Jim Harrison, one of the seven gunmen Crawford had hired two years ago to rid his range of nesters and rustlers. A big man on a gray Arabian with a Mexican saddle crusted with silver, he was one of the seven Crawford had sent out to deal with the Gypsies.

"What do you have, Jim?"

"Found Stillman snooping around again. At the Gypsy camp this time," Harrison said, using a gloved finger to wring the sweat from his handlebar mustache. "Apparently, he didn't heed our warning."

Crawford's voice was a blunt knife. "Damnit!"

Harrison lifted a hand. "Not to worry. We took care of him. No one will ever find him. You know that cave tucked back in that hollow east of Handren Hill?"

"You put him there?"

"He put himself there." Harrison rearranged himself in his saddle, a smirk lighting his eyes.

The three men behind him grinned.

"What the hell are you talking about, Jim?"

"He ran to ground there, and we pushed the mountain down on top of him. Wasn't hard to get a rockslide going with all those loose boulders hanging off that lip. Sealed the cave up tighter than a schoolmarm's lap."

Harrison turned a look at his comrades, laughing and shaking his head. Then a thought sobered him, and he looked at Crawford, who was still mulling the idea of Stillman's death.

"Oh," Harrison said. 'The woman... uh, what was her name—Tobias?—she was with him."

Crawford lifted a sharp look at the gunman. "Nell Tobias?"

Harrison didn't say anything. He sat on the Arabian, gauging his boss's reaction to the news that he'd killed the woman Crawford had tried to marry.

"What the hell was she doing with Stillman?" Crawford asked, his face even redder than usual, his exasperation flavored with jealousy.

"I don't know, sir," Harrison said with a shrug. "They

were in a wagon together. We seen 'em as they were leaving that ravine we buried the Gypsies in."

Crawford averted his gaze, pondering the information. His voice was speculative. "He must've found her... or she found him... after you boys rode roughshod on him."

"I reckon so, sir. Mr. Crawford, I didn't see no other way. I mean, she was there with him. She must've shown him the ravine..."

"So she must've known about the Gypsies," Crawford pondered. His mind was working it over as he inspected the painted porch boards around his boots. Her ranch was near the Gypsy camp. She'd probably heard the shots and come snooping, and then gone to town for Boomhauer.

Harrison said, "I'm sorry, Mr. Crawford. I didn't see no other way."

Crawford scratched his head, thinking it over. Finally, a grin pulled at the corners of his rigid mouth. "No, that's okay, Jim. You had to do what you had to do. That's what I pay you for. You boys go on back to the bunkhouse. Have the cook fry you up some steaks, and get you a good night's sleep. You deserve it."

The four men studied him guardedly. Finally, Harrison smiled, touched his hat brim, and reined his horse away from the porch. "Thank you, sir. Good night."

"Good night Jim."

The other men said good night and Crawford replied in kind, watching them walk their horses down the hill to the corrals.

Feeling a grim satisfaction, the rancher fished a fat brandy-soaked stogie from the breast pocket of his coat, nipped off the twist at the end, and lit up. Not only was Stillman out of the way, where no one could find the body or link his murder to Crawford, the Tobias widow was dead as well.

The woman had not only spurned Crawford—him, the biggest rancher in the county!—but she'd refused to sell her land to him. Served the high-headed filly right to be entombed in that mountain. Now the kid and his idiot uncle will pull out, leave their land and water to Crawford.

Yes, things had turned out just fine.

Feeling plucky, Crawford strode off the porch to the fine rosewood bay gelding he'd had one of the men lead up to the house. He untied the reins from the tie rail and mounted. Puffing the stogie, he' reined the high-stepping horse away from the hitch rack. Realizing his bodyguard had not yet appeared, he jerked a look at the group gathered around the corral. He was about to yell for Curtis when he saw the man gallop his horse out of the main barn, heading toward him.

"It's about time," Crawford groused with little venom. Nothing could destroy his good feeling about Stillman's and the widow's demise. "I called for you a half hour ago."

"Sorry, Mr. Crawford," Curtis said, his anvil chin drooping.

He was a simpleton, Curtis was, but he was big, he loved to fight, and he was good with a gun. And he was unwaveringly loyal to the man who signed his paychecks. All in all, Curtis Clemens was the best bodyguard a man could ask for. Crawford needed a big, dependable bodyguard, for a man did not attain his wealth and power without accruing a few enemies.

"Lonny bet me I couldn't win him at arm-wrestlin' two out of three, and I showed him I could." Curtis chuckled his idiot's chuckle. "Dang near broke his wrist for him too, I did! Ha-ha!"

"Come along, Curtis, come along," Crawford said indulgently, heeling the rosewood bay onto the trail to town.

"What are we goin' to town for, Mr. Crawford?" the big idiot asked when he'd caught up to his boss.

"Well, I *was* going to town for a woman and a stud game at the Stockmen's, but now I really have something to celebrate, Curtis!" Crawford removed the cigar from his mouth, threw his head back, and guffawed. He spurred the big gelding into a gallop. "Now I really have something to celebrate!"

———

THE RIDE TOOK the men an hour and a half, and by the time they arrived in Lone Pine, the sun was down, though a sapphire glow remained along the western horizon. Crawford dismounted at the Stockmen's, and Curtis led the rosewood bay off to the livery barn. Both men would stay in town tonight, Crawford with a girl on the tavern's second floor while Curtis watched the stairs, and return to the ranch after breakfast in the morning.

While Curtis headed west down the street named after his boss, Crawford parted the Stockmen's batwings. A couple of townsmen and a waddy were trying their luck at the faro table, and the two Irish boys who ran the sawmill were playing pool, a frothy beer pitcher standing on a nearby table.

Two pleasure girls in spare, frilly dresses sat cross-legged at a table near the bar, where Wilfred Drake stood before a whiskey tumbler. A cigar smoldered between his pudgy fingers. One shiny brown shoe was hiked before the other, and Drake was standing sideways, his left elbow on the bar, a pensive mood wrinkling the corners of his eyes.

His gaze lifted when Crawford sauntered in, and his mouth turned down.

"Well, Max..." he said, trying to sound friendly.

He and Crawford shared ownership of the Stockmen's as well as a freighting company. The bank was all Drake's, but it never would have been possible without Crawford's initial backing and patronage. In turn, Drake owned a small share of the Snaketrack. It was purely a business arrangement; the men were not friends. They were too much alike in that each wanted everything for himself.

"Hello, Wilfred," Crawford said easily, smiling his slit-eyed smile. He removed his gloves and slapped them down on the bar. "Fancy meeting you here this time of the night I thought you spent the evenings with your wife and daughter. Reading and conversing in the parlor. That sort of civilized thing."

"Dory isn't feeling well," Drake said, ignoring Crawford's smirking tone and dropping his eyes to his drink.

"The wife feeling poorly, eh? Nothing serious, I hope?"

Drake shook his head. "Just nerves. The doctor's prescribed sedatives."

The barman had come down and stood across from Crawford, who ordered a rye. When the man had set it up, Crawford threw it back and plunked the empty glass on the bar, smacking his lips. "Hit me again, Ray. In fact, why don't you leave the bottle?"

"Yessir, Mr. Crawford," Ray said, and returned to his dishpan, where a large coffee pot awaited his scrubbing.

"What do you have to celebrate tonight, Max?" Drake asked, unable to conceal a note of disdain in his voice.

"We, Fred. It's what *we* have to celebrate." Crawford turned to one of the girls—a buxom brunette with round, red lips—at the table behind Drake. "Sally, go upstairs. I'll be up in a few minutes."

When the girl scraped her chair back, stood, and walked indolently toward the stairs, he turned back to his partner, who gazed at him, waiting.

"All right," Drake said. "You've piqued my curiosity. What do *we* have to celebrate, Max?"

Crawford took another drink. "Stillman's dead."

Drake looked around, his face mottling from his chin to deep in his widow's peak. His jowls quivered as he sidled up to Crawford with a conspiratorial air, keeping his impassioned voice low. "Not so loud, Max—for chrissakes!"

He glanced again at the bartender, then at the soiled dove sitting at the table her friend had vacated, nursing a beer. She gave Drake a wan, hopeful smile. The banker said, "Let's sit down," and headed for a table on the other side of the room, near the piano.

As Crawford, grinning like the lone cock in the henhouse, grabbed his bottle and glass and followed, Drake yanked out a chair and sat down. He hunched over his whiskey, tapping his fingers as he waited for the sauntering Crawford, who pulled out the chair beside Drake's and leisurely sank into it.

Drake asked with hushed anxiety, "Okay—what happened?"

Crawford shrugged and refilled his glass, then refilled Drake's. He set the bottle on the table and shrugged, smiling. "He's dead. What can I tell you? He didn't scare out of the country like we hoped, so he's dead."

"Stillman," Drake said, scratching his chin and mulling over the significance of the situation. He'd had a hand in murdering one of the most famous lawmen in the territory. "How? Damnit, now federals will come and start snooping around. You see, Max, this was what I was afraid of! They'll find his body, and then they'll find—!"

"What are you so hot about? You tried to have him killed just the other night."

"That was before I thought through all the possible

consequences. It was an impulsive move. Don't you see—if we kill him, they'll find the body—"

Crawford held up a lazy hand, cutting Drake off. He shook his head. "They won't find the body. My boys saw to that."

"Why? How?"

"Trust me."

"Trust you?" Drake had spoken too loudly. He looked around. The Irishmen playing pool had glanced his way. The banker turned back to Crawford and lowered his voice. "How can I trust you? You sent your men out after that Gypsy boy, and they ended up killing the whole damn bunch!"

"That wasn't their fault," Crawford said. "A couple of those Gypsies pulled pistols. They were the ones who started the shooting. My boys opened up on them in self-defense. Now, I'll admit they got a little carried away, but... have you ever been shot at, Fred?"

Drake did not respond to this. He sat staring down at his drink.

Watching him, gauging his mood, Crawford said, "Besides, you're the one who wanted us to go out there in the first place. You must remember that—don't you, Fred? I did it only as a personal favor to a business partner—"

"Yes, yes, I remember." Drake tossed his drink back and set the empty glass on the table. "I just can't cotton to the idea of killing another lawman." He reached for the bottle and filled his glass.

"Well, remember, Fred—lest you should forget—it wasn't me who killed the first one."

Drake whipped his sharp, rheumy gaze to Crawford. His broad nose was a maze of swollen blue veins. "I didn't have any choice! He was going out there, and when he got back he would have sent for the sheriff! And once the sheriff seen—saw—what happened, he would have called in federal marshals." Drake patted his hand on the table to emphasize his declaration. "Then you and I would both be finished!"

"Come now, Fred, don't get yourself all stirred up." Crawford patted his partner's hand indulgently, and his voice had a chill in it. "Emotional men make mistakes. Especially ones with sick wives and daughters who... well—"

"Get your filthy mouth off my daughter or I'll—!"

"You'll what?" The grin remained on Crawford's lips, but his eyes were at once dull and hard. He leaned into Drake. "Remember, Fred. You need me much more than I need you. My ranch is free and clear. I pay cash on the barrelhead for everything, and I can buy your share, of this place and the freighting outfit here and now if you like. Here and now."

He sidled even closer so that Drake could smell the trail sweat and rye. "But without me, you're nothing. Just another Crawford Street drummer at the mercy of Lone Pine's boom-and-bust market, which sneezes when I do and wipes my nose. I could put up another bank and close you down so fast it would make your head spin."

Crawford pulled away, tossed back his drink, grabbed his gloves, and shoved his chair back. "Now if you'll excuse me, Sally's waiting for me upstairs."

The tall rancher started away, stopped, and turned back. A hand on Drake's chair back, he crouched down so his voice would not be heard above the saloon's desultory chatter and the intermittent clatter of pool balls.

"Oh, one more piece of news," he said softly. "The Widow Tobias has tragically disappeared as well. She was with Stillman. So, that business of calling her bank loans due, which I believe we discussed a few weeks ago, will no longer be necessary."

With another grin, he placed a big hand on his partner's shoulder and squeezed till Drake winced from the pain. Then the rancher turned and headed for the stairs.

Drake sat in shock, vaguely rubbing his shoulder. Nell Tobias dead, too. How many more would die before this thing was over?

Would it ever be over? Was there ever a conclusion to trouble as ghastly as this? Trouble that seemed to take on a life of its own, reproducing itself over and over?

If only Sybil hadn't met that boy... oh, Jesus...!

Drake saw someone looking at him. It was Crawford's bodyguard, Curtis Clemens. The big man in trail clothes sat in a chair beside the pleasure girl, at the table near the bar, his dusty Stetson tipped back on his head. The girl's hand was on his knee, and she was talking to him seductively, but Curtis was watching Drake. He grinned his sycophant's idiot grin. Raising his glass in salute, he winked at Drake and drank.

Then he turned his attention to the girl. Feeling suddenly sick, Drake stood and made for the door. As he parted the batwings and stepped onto the boardwalk, he nearly ran into the big, slouching figure of Nick Corey.

"Oh, hi, Mr. Drake!" Corey said. "How are you doin' this wonderful evenin'?"

Drake gasped, grumbled, and stepped around the big deputy, donning his crisp bowler and hurrying off down the boardwalk.

Chapter Fourteen

THAT NIGHT STILLMAN woke to the cave floor shaking and rumbling. His head was heavy from lack of oxygen, however, and he quickly fell back asleep, his chin on his neck.

The next morning, he woke with a start. Looking around, he remembered where he was. Nell slept with her head on his thigh, her hair in disarray, her legs curled like a child's.

Stillman sighed and reclined his head against the cave wall. He closed his eyes. Then he opened them. He looked at Nell again, seeing her dimly. Looking up, he could see the pocked stone wall before him.

The dark of the cave was not as dark as before. How could that be?

He swung his head left, and lightning surged through him, numbing the pain of his bruised ribs. Far back in the corridor, a sliver of wan morning light shone.

What the hell?

He sniffed the air. It was fresh, smelling faintly of dew and pine.

Stillman shook the woman and grabbed his rifle. "Nell."

When she groaned and lifted her head, he climbed stiffly to his feet. He reached down for her arm.

"Nell, come on."

"What is it?"

"Look."

Silently, holding hands, they walked toward the light, stepping over stones that had fallen from the ceiling or heaved up from the floor. The fissure was so narrow that they had to pass in single file. Twice it narrowed so much they had to squeeze through. Stillman crouched, for the ceiling was low.

The air smelled fresher with every step they took.

Finally, they approached the opening—a six-by-two-inch crack between rocks about six feet up from the ground.

"Well, I'll be," Stillman mused. "I heard rumbling last night Must've been another rock slide. And damn if it didn't open a back door."

Nell's voice quavered with jubilant expectation. "Can we get through?"

Stillman was probing the crack with his fingers, testing the rocks on both sides. "Stand back," he said. "Far back. These rocks could come in on top of us."

When he'd tested the weight of each stone around the crack, seeing which ones had the most give, he reached up with both hands on one and shoved. It gave, rolling away, opening the crack another six inches, bathing Stillman's craggy face with salmon light and fresh, dewy air.

He could hear birds hunting in the rookery for breakfast He'd never heard anything so sweet

"Oh, my God," Nell said through a gasp.

"Well, that's one down." Stillman tested another stone

with his fingers, trying to decide which way it would go if he shoved—down or out?

He shoved. The stone dislodged slowly after Stillman had rolled up on his toes, heaving. It clattered heavily down the mountain. Its absence widened the hole by another half foot so that it was now about as big around as a milk pail.

He probed another rock, placed both hands on it, and heaved. He'd gotten it lifted and nearly removed when it plunged straight down—with several more behind it. The rocks poured out of the ceiling as though from a chute.

Nell screamed as Stillman twisted around, trying to get out of the way, and fell on his side, the rocks landing around his legs and waist. He covered his head with his arms, expecting the whole ceiling to thunder down on top of him, but a sudden silence rose as the dust wafted and began settling.

Stillman removed his arms from his face. Through the new opening, the circumference of a well hole, he could see a great curve of sky sliced by bird wings. Nell ran to him, "Ben—are you all right?"

He moved his legs, around which the rocks had formed a cairn. "I think so."

Nell rolled a stone off the small heap, freeing one leg, which Stillman lifted and used to free the other. Pushing himself up with his hands, he gained his knees, testing his legs with his weight, and stood. Grunting, he said, "Just bruised. Let's get the hell out of here."

The hole was now several feet lower than it had been, and Stillman hoisted himself out relatively easily. He turned and offered Nell his hand. She looked up at him from what had nearly been their crypt.

"Your ribs," she protested.

Stillman shook his head. "The ribs are fine." They

were. He'd probably feel them later, but at the moment they were quiet as sleeping babes.

When he'd helped Nell through the hole, she gained her feet and stood grinning at him. Stillman smiled back and turned to look over the valley, where the dawn hung like blue, sun-mottled fog, the pines and aspens slowly separating from the lifting shadows.

He took several deep breaths and turned to Nell, who stared down the mountain, awestruck, inhaling and exhaling like she'd never tasted air so sweet. She turned to him, her tawny eyes shining, wisps of loose hair caressing her lovely face. She threw her arms around him, her body wracked with sobs of joy. He held her tightly, his cheek against her head, running his hands across her back.

She drew away from him, looked into his eyes, and kissed him. Her lips were full and warm and silky as they moved against his, parting. He felt her bosom swell against his chest. She drew up on the toes of her boots, encircling her arms about his neck, kissing him hungrily, pressing against him with unfettered passion.

Finally, her body relaxed and their lips separated. He stared into her eyes, his mind a nest of conflicting emotions —aroused, revolted, ashamed. She stared back as slowly the flush of passion faded from her face. Seeing his expression, she dropped her gaze, darkening with chagrin.

She swallowed. "I'm sorry."

He studied her, troubled, his emotions settling like the flames after an explosion. He stood, retrieving his rifle, and took her hand. "Come on."

Hand-in-hand, they slowly made their way down the rock-strewn mountain to a creek threading through the trees at the valley's bottom. They dropped to their knees and drank, scrubbing their faces in the steely-cool water as it tinkled over moss-furred stones.

"You know how to get back to your ranch?" Stillman asked Nell.

"All I know is that, since the sun's rising there, it's that way. But I've never been in this valley before. If we head east, though, we should hook up with the Sugar Creek trail. That'll take us to within a mile of the ranch."

Stillman nodded. "Well, you ready to walk?"

"I'm so happy to be alive," Nell said, splashing one more handful of water on her face, "that I could run."

"I know what you mean."

She looked at him, water trickling down her face, wet wisps of hair plastered to her skin. "We were pretty close to it, weren't we?"

Chuckling, Stillman ran a hand through his wet hair. He grinned ruefully, squinting an eye. "Well, let's just say we were holding quite a few deuces there for a while."

"Won't the Snaketrack men be surprised."

Stillman chuckled at that too and shook his head. "Yeah, but let's just hope they don't find out we're still kickin'" before we're ready for them."

"What are you going to do?"

"As soon I can, I'm gonna head to town and send wires out to the Blaine County sheriff and the marshal's office down in Helena. I have a few other things I want to look into too."

"Lone Pine's a dangerous place these days," Nell warned.

"I'll be watching my backside." Stillman donned his hat and stood. He offered his hand. "We best get moving.

———

TWO HOURS LATER, after stopping twice for rests and water, they walked along the Sugar Creek trail, a bright sun overhead. Two horseback riders appeared on the flat to their left, cantering toward them through a scattered herd of grazing cattle.

Stillman grabbed Nell's arm protectively and raised his rifle.

The smallest of the two riders, breaking into a gallop, called, "Ma!"

"It's Robbie and Limon!" Nell cried. She lifted an arm and waved excitedly, laughing. She ran out in the flat to meet the boy, who galloped in, slid expertly out of the leather, and ran into his mother's waiting arms.

"Oh, Robbie!"

"Ma! We thought you was dead, Ma!"

"Oh, I'm so sorry to worry you, son," Nell said, on her knees and rocking the boy back and forth in her arms.

Limon cantered up, his eyes wide and shiny beneath the brim of his straw hat. He shook his head darkly. "We sure was powerful worried about you two. Ole Demon, he come home yesterday noon looking spooked as all get-out, and we just couldn't figure out what happened."

"Snaketrack riders threw us a loop," Stillman explained.

Limon winced like he'd swallowed something sour. "We tracked you out to that ravine... but the sign got all jumbled after that. I never been much of a tracker."

Stillman smiled at the timid, unconfident man. "You did all right, Limon. We're mighty glad to see you."

"I hope you have some birds at home," Nell said, playfully giving Robbie's blond hair a ruffle. "I'm about as hungry as I've ever been."

Stillman mounted Robbie's horse, giving the boy a hand up behind him, and Nell mounted behind Limon. They cantered into the ranch yard a half hour later. It was late afternoon, shadows extending from the buildings and corral posts, and the golden air teemed with seed from the cottonwoods along the creek.

Stillman told Nell he'd be heading on to town—he was eager to get those wires off—and turned toward the corral, where Sweets watched him, thrusting his head over the split-rail fence. Nell's protest turned him back around.

"It's too late in the day to start for town," she said. "You won't get there till after dark, and the Western Union office will be closed anyway. Besides that, look at you. You're tired and hungry."

She grabbed his arm and pulled him toward the cabin. "Oh, no, you don't, Ben Stillman. You're gonna have a bath, and I'm going to rewrap those ribs. Then you're going to sit down for a civilized meal at my kitchen table. Tomorrow is soon enough for sending your wires."

Stillman was tired and hungry enough to let himself be led. On the porch, they stopped and turned to each other. Placing his hands on her shoulders, Stillman said, "Mrs. Tobias, your charm is equaled only by your hospitality."

Her gaze had a pensive depth as she placed her hands on either side of his rugged, unshaven face and stared deeply into his eyes. Her own eyes had a troubled cast as she turned away, opened the screen door, and disappeared inside.

With a sigh, Stillman turned toward the yard, placing a hand on one of the support posts. He watched Limon forking hay into the corral. Robbie lugged two sloshing water buckets from the windmill.

Stillman saw neither of them; his mind turned inward...

Later that night, in spite of his exhaustion and sore ribs, he tossed and turned in bed. Finally, he got up, dressed in his jeans and shirt, and padded barefoot out to the kitchen, where he pumped water into a cup. He went out to the porch and sat in one of the hide-bottom chairs.

He built a cigarette and sat smoking and sipping the water, staring out at the ranch yard lit by a pearl half-moon rising over the eastern hogbacks. He thought about himself and Fay, and then he thought about Nell, remembering the stolen kiss on the mountain. He did not like remembering the kiss, because it filled him with remorse, but he remembered it anyway, in all its details—the warm, wet feel of her lips against his...

The remorse was tempered with desire, and then the remorse returned, even stronger than before.

Finally, he finished his water and the quirley and went back inside. He refilled the cup at the pump before heading back to his room, steering around the rough-hewn furniture by the moonlight slanting through windows.

When he was almost to his room, he heard a click. The door beside his opened. He knew it was the door to Nell's room, and she stood in the half-open door, silhouetted by the milky light washing through the window behind her. Her hair fell about her shoulders. She wore a white-lace wrapper.

Stillman stood frozen, watching her. She said nothing, and neither did he. His heart heaved, pain racked his ribs, and his breath was tight in his throat. Part of him wanted to go to her, but the part that did not—could not—shoved him toward his own door. He went inside the room and closed the door softly behind him.

He listened for a moment. A hinge squeaked as Nell closed her door, the bolt catching in the latch with a click.

The next morning, Stillman and Nell pretended nothing had happened, and after breakfast, Stillman saddled Sweets in the barn. He came back into the cabin for his rifle and saddlebags and saw her washing dishes at the range. Robbie stood beside her, drying the dishes and putting them away. Limon was outside greasing a hay mower.

His rifle in his hand and his saddlebags draped over the other shoulder, Stillman stopped in the kitchen. He cleared his throat and said, "I reckon I'll be leavin'."

She turned to him, drying her hands on a dishtowel.

"Good-bye, Mr. Stillman," Robbie said. "It was nice meeting you, sir."

Stillman smiled and shook the boy's hand. "The pleasure was mine, Robbie. Thanks again for saving my hide the other day."

The boy blushed. "Ah, it wasn't nothin'," he said. "Just lucky I was around, I reckon."

"I reckon I was at that," Stillman agreed.

He looked at Nell, who dropped her eyes, flushing. He turned, pushed through the screen, and walked over to his horse, tied to the corral by the barn. He draped the bags behind his saddle and bedroll and slid his rifle into the boot.

"Good-bye, Mr. Stillman," Limon called from the other side of the corral, where he was greasing the gears on the mower.

Stillman saluted the man and turned a stirrup out. Before he could poke his boot through the stirrup, he heard the screen door slap shut and turned to watch Nell approach across the yard. She was carrying a small flour sack tied at the top with a rawhide cord.

"I almost forgot," she said, approaching. "I packed a lunch for you. Bacon biscuits and some deer jerky. For the ride to town, in case the breakfast wasn't enough."

"I can't imagine one of your breakfasts not being enough," Stillman said, accepting the gift, "but I'm obliged."

She was silent, her eyes downcast. Stillman waited, knowing she had something to say.

She lifted her gaze to his, swallowed, and licked her lips. "I'm sorry," she said, haltingly. "I never thought of myself as the sort... the sort of woman who would tempt a married man."

Stillman turned and tied the food sack to his saddle. "Well, I never thought of myself as the type of married man who could be tempted." He turned to her again. "Until I met you."

"I hope you don't think ill of me."

Stillman shook his head. "Not by a long shot." He took her in his arms and hugged her. He held her tightly, feeling her shoulders jerk with a sob.

"You be careful in town," she said as he mounted. "There's danger there. Don't do anything until you have help."

"I'll watch my backside," Stillman said, touching his hat brim and smiling in spite of himself. "You take care."

He reached out for her hand and held it for several seconds, staring into her tear-glazed eyes with a gentle smile. Then he toed the bay to a gallop, and Nell watched him go, looking worried as she shielded the morning sun from her eyes with her hand.

"You too, Ben. You too."

Chapter Fifteen

STILLMAN MADE IT to Lone Pine by noon.

He stabled Sweets at the livery barn, assuring the cow-eyed proprietor he'd be held personally responsible for the horse's safety. Then he headed for the Western Union office.

He'd walked a quarter block when he saw Nick Corey headed in the same direction, ahead of Stillman and on the other side of the street. Stillman stopped and paused behind an awning post

Corey no doubt thought the Hill County sheriff was dead, and Stillman wanted Lone Pine's illustrious lawman to go on believing just that—at least until he'd sent his telegrams. Which meant he'd have to delay his visit to the Western Union office until Corey had wandered back to his office and his pile of illustrated magazines.

Frustrated, Stillman walked to the Maclean House with his saddlebags and rifle. The old proprietor looked none too happy to see him. With a sigh, he merely twirled the ledger book so Stillman could sign his name, and handed over the key to the same room Stillman had occupied a few days ago.

As Stillman headed for the stairs, old Maclean grumbled ruefully, "Looks like you tied into the wrong bunch of polecats."

Knowing the old man had seen the bruises on his face, Stillman said, "We were just gettin' acquainted." On the stairs, he turned to the hotelkeeper, as if an afterthought. "Say, would you send your granddaughter up with some hot water? Rachel's her name, isn't it? I'd like to scrub this trail dust off my hide."

"I gave her a couple hours off," the old man said testily. "I'll send her up when she gets back. My days of luggin' water up those steps ended ten years ago."

Stillman winked and continued up the stairs to his room. He tossed his saddlebags over a chair and propped his rifle beside the washstand. He didn't want the bath; he wanted to talk to the girl. When she'd spoken to him before, she'd mentioned the Gypsies and a friend. Now, in light of the Gypsies' murder, he was more curious than ever about what she'd started to tell him.

He knew the information could wait. This was not technically his investigation. Nevertheless, his curiosity kept him in the warm room, stretched out in the bed, waiting for the girl while listening to a fly buzz against the window. The puzzle had seemed to piece together in his mind, but one piece was missing, and he had a strong suspicion Maclean's granddaughter was holding it.

Finally, when he'd decided she wasn't going to show, he retrieved a battered notebook from his saddlebags and scribbled out three telegrams—one to the sheriff in Chinook, one to the United States Marshal's office in Helena, and one to his wife, Fay, informing her he was all right and that he'd be home soon.

Then he grabbed his hat and headed down the hotel's back stairs.

He took as secluded a route as possible to the Western Union office, wanting to avoid Corey and Drake until the messages had been safely sent. He knew the fact that he'd sent for help would spread from the telegraph office like wildfire, and that was fine with him. Once Drake, Corey, and Crawford knew Stillman had help on the way, they'd think twice before moving against him again. He'd named all three as suspects in his telegrams, so they'd be the first to be investigated in the event of his demise.

He doubted they'd run. Doing so would only prove their guilt.

At the Western Union office, he interrupted the telegrapher's lunch. Chewing, the corpulent man rose from his cluttered table and entered the telegraph cage, adjusting his green eyeshade and wiping his greasy hands on his trousers. With a pudgy finger, he nudged his spectacles up his nose and stared at Stillman's three notes with a sigh.

When he'd finished reading the first two missives, his face was as red as a July Fourth bonfire. Perspiration beaded on his forehead.

"Are you sure... you sure you want to send these, Mr. Stillman?"

"Send 'em."

The man's face was pained, his voice mournful. "But... why, I don't believe Mr. Drake and Mr.—"

"Send 'em," Stillman ordered, his eyes hard and authoritative.

He stood there while the flustered telegrapher clicked reluctantly away on the key. When the man finished, shaking his head and glancing sidelong at the bank across the street, Stillman paid him and wandered east up Crawford Street, knowing that he wouldn't be a block away before the telegrapher had started spreading the news.

Stillman didn't know how much the citizens of Lone Pine knew about the murder of the Gypsies and of Charlie Boomhauer—probably very little when you got right down to it—but they obviously knew something was amiss. They'd learned not to say much, with a reprobate like Nicky Corey packing a badge.

When the news that lawmen with jurisdiction were on the way to investigate the town marshal, Lone Pine's lone banker and the area's most prominent cattleman, the town would be in an uproar. It might even cause a run on the bank, which could devastate not only the town but most of the farmers and ranchers in the area. Such a possibility was probably another reason why the citizens had played dumb to Stillman's previous inquiries.

It wasn't a good situation for the town, but murder never was. Lone Pine would recover—if it grew a spine and the guts to go with it, that is. Sometimes you had to stand up for what's right, money and comfort be damned.

Stillman came to the corner and glanced at the bank. He hadn't met Drake yet. Why not introduce himself now? Drake would learn soon enough that Stillman was alive.

He started for the bank but paused when he saw the telegrapher heading in the same direction, crossing Crawford Street to Stillman's right

"I'll give him the message," Stillman called to the man with a devilish wink.

The telegrapher stopped in the street flushing and scowling, then turned and headed sheepishly back toward his office.

Stillman had been in enough banks to know what the president's door looked like. He knocked once and entered.

"Just a moment," Drake said impatiently. He was

standing before a bookcase on the other side of his massive desk, his back to Stillman as he perused the heavy tome in his hands.

Stillman smiled and crossed his arms over his chest waiting. Finally, Drake returned his book to the case, and turned, saying haughtily, "Yes, what is it?"

Stillman grinned with mock friendliness. "Hello, Mr. Drake. I'm Ben Stillman. I just wanted to stop in and introduce myself."

Gripped as if by a seizure, Drake grabbed his chest and staggered back against the bookcase. He tried to speak but emitted only choking sounds.

"You all right?" Stillman asked, rushing to the man with mock concern. "Here, you better sit down before you pass out." He guided the stricken Drake to his padded-leather chair. "There you go, take a load off your feet. Sir, you don't look well. Are you sure you're all right?"

Stillman patted the banker on his back, then reached for the brandy decanter. He splashed some brandy in a glass and offered the glass to Drake.

"Here you go—have you a sip of that. Nothing better for the ticker than a good, stiff drink—that's what my own Doc Evans always says."

Drake accepted the glass and took a healthy slug, wincing as it went down his throat. His rheumy eyes found Stillman, scouring the lawman as if searching for something in his clothes. His face slackened, and he dropped his gaze.

"Thanks, thanks," he said. "Don't know what happened there. Better... better see the doc, I reckon..."

Stillman chuckled. "I think you'd better. Such a reaction could be an indication of a major health problem." He moved back around to the front of the desk and slacked into a chair. "Unless, of course, you were just

surprised to see me. Maybe you'd heard I was dead—
buried in some cave out yonder with Nell Tobias.
Murdered."

Drake had taken another mournful of the liquor, and
he swallowed it hard, flushing all over again, and slumped
back in his chair, trying to arrange a guileless, puzzled
expression. He cleared his throat. "I'm afraid I don't know
what you're talking about, Sheriff."

Stillman's smile evaporated. His voice tightened. "Yes,
you do," he said, placing his hat on his knee and staring
hard at the banker. "I had my doubts before I came in
here. But after seeing your reaction to my living, breathing
face, there's no longer any doubt in my mind that you're
involved in the killings. In fact, if trouble were quicksand,
you'd be floating belly-down in it."

He let this wash over Drake, who sat slouched and
staring back at him dully.

"What I want to know is how are you involved? Did
Crawford kill the Gypsies and then you ordered
Boomhauer killed to cover Crawford's tail, or did it happen
some other way?"

He waited. Drake just stared at him, breathing through
his slitted mouth, color playing up from his jowls and
changing hues, the light from the window behind Stillman
glinting in his glasses.

"Or are you behind the whole thing? Did you have the
Gypsies killed? Why?"

Drake straightened in his chair and bellied up to the
desk. He appeared calm at last, but his soft hands quivered
slightly. "You're fishing, Stillman. I don't know what you're
talking about. Why would I have the Gypsies killed? Why
would I have Boomhauer killed? He was the marshal here,
for godsakes. I'm a law-abiding man. Now, if you'll excuse
me, you're out of your jurisdiction, and I have work to do."

"Well, I'll let you get back to it," Stillman said. "But before I do, I want you to keep this in mind. I've sent for the county sheriff and federal marshals. They're on the way here. Now, it might take them a day or two to get here, but when they do, we'll be making a thorough investigation. I already have enough evidence to hang Crawford and his gunslicks from one of those big cottonwoods along the creek yonder. I don't have any hard evidence on you and Corey yet, but it's been my experience that when one of the guilty starts to talk—for a more lenient sentence, say, or just so they won't be swingin' alone from that cottonwood branch—we'll have enough on you two as well."

"Get out of my office!"

Calmly, Stillman raised a hand for quiet. "And one other thing." He leaned forward in his chair, his hat in his hands, staring menacingly at Drake over the hide-covered surface of the massive desk. "If, between now and when the other lawmen get here, you sic the dogs on me, you better hope like hell they don't botch the job again. Because if they do, I'll be payin' you another visit, and I won't be near so sweet as I've been here today."

With that, Stillman winked, stood, and walked to the door. He opened it, said, "Good day, Mr. Drake," and donned his hat and left.

Behind him, Drake smoldered in his chair, staring at the door. Finally, with trembling hands, he poured himself another drink and slammed it back.

As Stillman headed eastward on the splintery sidewalk, his heart thumping with the vexing but decisive knowledge that Drake too was involved in the killings, he stopped suddenly when he saw Maclean's granddaughter heading south on Montana Avenue. From the dust on her shoes and gray skirts, it looked as though she'd walked quite a ways.

Stillman watched her pass before him, crossing Craw-

ford and continuing toward the creek and her grandparents' hotel beyond. He began walking quickly, to catch up
to her but stopped again when she stopped and turned to
face the alley behind the mercantile.

She stood for several seconds as if frozen. Then she
backed up slowly, shaking her head from side to side. A
man bolted out from behind the mercantile—a big man in
a deer-hide vest. He grabbed the girl and jerked her,
screaming and fighting, into the alley.

Stillman ran.

Chapter Sixteen

AT THE ALLEY'S MOUTH, STILLMAN WHEELED LEFT.

Before him, Nick Corey had the girl in a bear hug from behind. As he shuffled sideways, dragging the girl farther back into the alley's thickening shadows, he nuzzled her neck. A look of animal lust and fury mottled his face. His hat had fallen off, and a wing of sandy hair flopped over his eyes.

As Stillman started toward them, the girl lifted her right foot and brought the heel down hard on one of Corey's soft boots.

"Ah—you *bitch!*"

She slipped from his flagging grasp, but before she could get clear, he grabbed her dress, ripping it off her shoulder and jerking her toward him. He slapped her across the face. With a scream, the girl fell against a stack of empty shipping crates.

Corey saw Stillman out of the corner of his eye and wheeled toward him. The marshal froze. His jaw fell, and his eyes flashed unfettered shock.

"What's the matter, Nick—see a ghost?"

Corey's lips moved soundlessly, his eyes narrowing. "You... what... you're... *dead!*"

"Not by a long shot." Stillman's hand was on his holstered gun, but he did not draw the weapon. "So, you're a pervert too, along with everything else—including the killer of Charlie Boomhauer."

The girl sobbed as she climbed to her feet, holding her torn dress closed. Keeping his eyes on Corey, Stillman said, "Go on home, Rachel."

The girl stood clumsily, jostling the crates, and ran out of the alley.

Stillman and Corey stared at each other. In Corey's eyes, astonishment transformed to cold cunning, the thin lips drawing up slightly at the corners. He opened his hand and moved it to the six-shooter on his right hip.

"Do it, Nick," Stillman said, his voice hard with unmasked hate. "I'd love you to do it. Save me a lot of trouble."

Corey's hand froze. He stood regarding Stillman with barely suppressed rage.

Stillman barked, "Draw!"

Corey grinned and let his hand fall from his holster. Suddenly he lowered his head and bulled toward Stillman, who'd seen it coming and sidestepped, drawing abreast of the marshal, grabbing the back of Corey's collar and heaving him into the street beyond the alley's mouth.

When he swung that, Stillman saw several townsmen gathered there, having probably heard the girl's scream. Others were on the way—men in aprons and shirtsleeves, a few drovers from the saloons—filtering down from Crawford Street.

Looking indignant, Corey climbed to his feet, wearing

the blond dust of the avenue. His jaw was taut, his teeth bared, his eyes narrow as rifle ports. He worked his raised fists in circles, moving sideways, his eyes fastened on Stillman, who raised his own hands and balled them, crouching.

Anger filled Stillman—the hot, compounding pressure of burning wrath. This man had murdered Charlie Boomhauer and had become a veritable wolf in the fold of Lone Pine. This man—this wretched underling of corrupt and powerful men.

Corey darted toward Stillman and swung a round-house. Stillman ducked, pivoted, jabbed Corey twice in the belly, and as the marshal lowered his hands, recovering from the blows that had pummeled the breath from his lungs, Stillman rammed his right fist against Corey's left cheekbone. Corey staggered backward. Before he could regain his balance, Stillman bolted forward and hit him again in the jaw.

Corey fell but scampered immediately back to his feet, crouching and facing Stillman, his eyes savage, blood leaking from his cut chin. Stillman moved in again, but Corey was ready for him this time, blocking Stillman's hook with a forearm and smacking Stillman's cheek with a hard jab. The blow jarred Stillman clear down to his heels, and he winced as he rocked sideways, avoiding the long roundhouse Corey swung. When Corey's fist had skimmed Stillman's face, Stillman swung his own roundhouse. Before he could land it, Corey jabbed his jaw.

Surprised by the blow, which rattled his teeth and reopened a cut, Stillman shuffled backward, his face stinging. Corey followed and came in low, swinging his head and both arms, winding up with a haymaker.

Stillman ducked it and came back up swinging a hard

right into Corey's ear, tearing it. Corey gave a pained grunt, wincing, and while his eyes were still closed, Stillman hit him with his left, then the right again, and Corey fell on his back.

The Lone Pine marshal lifted his head, glaring.

Stillman stood over him, crouched and ready with his fists high. "What's the matter, Nick?" he asked tauntingly, knowing the man's ego was his softest spot. "I have fifteen years on you. What kind of a fighter are you anyway, can't take an old man?"

Corey heaved himself to his feet, his ear bleeding onto his collar, the gash in his chin leaking in earnest. He crouched and glowered, his jaw set again, but Stillman could see the pain and doubt in his eyes, see the wariness in his heavy-footed stance.

Sucking wind and swearing raspily, Corey swung. Stillman ducked and buried his right in the marshal's belly. Grunting but keeping his fists raised, Corey lifted his head and faded back, gathering his legs beneath him. He lowered his head and charged. Stillman crouched, side-stepped, and spun the marshal around with a stiff upper-cut. He followed it with a hard right to his temple, splitting the skin and drawing more blood.

Corey shook himself like a dog crawling out of a slough, cursed again in a hard blow of furious wind, and spun back around, facing Stillman. His chest heaved, and his hair was sweat-glued to his forehead.

His eyes raked the crowd of ten or so people who'd gathered around them, watching with mute interest, poker-faced. Flushing with chagrin, Corey jumped toward Still-man, faked a right, and swung his left. Reading the fake, Stillman landed a crushing roundhouse on Corey's left temple, where he'd hit him before, opening the gash even wider. Corey twirled, knees giving, and dropped. He lay there, heaving, spitting dust.

Stillman stood over him, feet spread. "I think you've gotten soft, Nick," he taunted. "Sittin' around the office all day, reading lurid magazines..."

"Da—" Corey tried hoarsely, heaving onto his elbows. "Damn you..."

'That's no way to talk, Nick." Stillman prodded the man with his boot toe. "Come on. Stand up and fight me, you foulmouthed coward."

Corey glowered at him over his shoulder. Then he climbed to his knees, from his knees to his feet. As he turned to face his opponent, he kept his head bowed, and Stillman knew what was on his mind even before the marshal's right hand clawed iron.

Corey's hand was rising when Stillman lunged toward him, kicking the .45 over Corey's head. Before the revolver had even reached the apex of its arc, Stillman gave the dumbfounded man a jaw-rattling backhand. He brought the same hand back, open palmed, against Corey's other cheek, jerking the exhausted man back the other way, reeling and tripping over his own boots.

Stillman finished his opponent off with a stiff uppercut that started from the ground. It buried Corey face-deep in the street. Corey's arms and legs, spread as though he'd fallen from the sky, tensed, then relaxed. He was out cold.

Stillman grabbed his shirt collar and dragged him like a hay bale through the parting crowd to the horse trough up by the mercantile. He jerked the unconscious marshal's shoulders up against the trough, planted his hand against the back of Corey's head, and plunged it face-first into the tepid water. He held it there until Corey started to fight, flailing with his arms and blowing bubbles.

Then Stillman let him go and walked back toward the alley for Corey's gun. The crowd had backed up to include the broader field of action in their scrutiny, and they watched Stillman like they were observing a rogue grizzly cross a meadow.

Gun in hand, Stillman tramped back to the half-conscious marshal. He opened the cylinder, shook out the shells, and tossed the gun into the trough behind Corey's head. It plopped and was gone.

Corey's head lolled on his shoulders, his back to the trough, his hair plastered to his head, his features creased with pain. Stillman watched him with enough anger to keep at him with his fists. He considered throwing the man in his own jail but decided against it. Such a move

would only provoke Drake and Crawford, and Stillman didn't want them provoked before he had a few more players on his team.

"That's for when you tried to drygulch me the other night, Nick," Stillman said. "And for the hoorawing party you directed me to the other day. When you want to dance again, let me know. You try back shooting me again, you yellow slime, I'll blow your worthless head off."

He started away, and stopped, turning back. "And when you hang, it'll be for Charlie."

———

COREY'S EARS TOLLED, the blood rushing in his head, his brain throbbing. Shame burned up from his bowels.

When he opened his swollen eyes, he saw that Stillman was gone and that most of the crowd had dispersed. But three drovers still watched from the corner opposite the mercantile.

With a preliminary effort at finding his voice, Corey yelled, "What the hell you lookin' at? Git... git the hell outta here!" He hated the womanish way his battered voice sounded and fought to contain an enraged sob.

He gritted his teeth against the spikes his yelling had driven between his ears, and reeled sideways, nearly passing out. He sat there grimly, rage intermittently flashing behind his mortified, unseeing gaze.

Finally, he turned clumsily, plunged his head into the horse trough, lifted it out, and feeling only slightly more alert, pushed himself to his feet. His legs were wobbly, and the blood still rushed painfully in his ears, but he began walking, heading for the west side of the avenue.

Staggering as though drunk, water and blood dripping on his already soaked shirt, he turned the corner around the millinery and shambled eastward down the boardwalk along Crawford Street. It was around four o'clock, and several shopkeepers were sweeping the walk-in preparation for closing their stores.

Corey pushed past them, not looking at them, his chest heaving, eyes glassy, his smashed lips set in a sneer.

When he came to the Lone Pine State Bank, he bulled through the door, turned left, and staggered through the gate in the wood fence. Everyone in the bank—customers, clerks, and tellers alike—froze when they saw him, watching with puzzled awe. No one said a word as he pushed through the heavy oak door at the building's rear, shuffled into the office, and slammed the door carelessly behind him.

In the office, Wilfred Drake sat behind his vast, cluttered desk, his jacket off and his sleeves rolled up his pale, pudgy forearms. A half-smoked cigar smoldered in a cut-glass ashtray.

The banker had looked up with anger when he'd heard

his door opening without even a cursory knock. Now his lips parted, and his jaw dropped as he watched Corey stagger in, looking like some beast of the forest, his face mangled, his wet shirt torn and mud-caked, his jeans coated with dust. Water dripped from the marshal's plastered hair to the expensive Oriental rug on the hardwood floor beneath his filthy boots.

Drake merely watched in silence as Corey, not so much as glancing at him, pounded over to the washstand. Breathing raspily and grunting painfully, Corey splashed water from the china pitcher, hung his head over the basin, and began bathing his face, wincing at the sting of his cuts. He grabbed a clean, white towel from the peg, soaked a corner in the water, and dabbed at the lacerations, scrutinizing his reflection in the glass-encased map of Montana Territory mounted above the stand.

Finally, Drake, sitting stiffly in his overstuffed chair but with color returning to his face, asked with a caustic grunt, "What in the hell happened to you?"

Corey took a few seconds before responding. "Stillman ain't dead. You told me he was dead."

Drake fell back in his chair, dropping his elbows to the armrests. "I just found out about it myself."

"Just found out about it yourself, huh?" Corey asked tonelessly, dabbing at the cuts in the map's reflection. "Well, why in the hell didn't you tell me?"

Drake lifted his stogie from the tray and gave it a considerate puff. He cared little for the underling's caustic tone, but decided to humor the man for the moment, and indulge in a little humor of his own. "It appears I didn't have to."

Corey winced as he dabbed a cut, and flushed at Drake's response. Immeasurably frustrated by the veritable crap-soup life had served him of late, Corey scrubbed his

hair with the dry end of the towel. Tossing the blood-splattered towel on its peg, he turned and walked to Drake's
desk, his eyes more surly now than deranged, and removed
the glass cork from the brandy decanter.

He splashed some in one of the matching goblets, then
flipped open the lid of Drake's carved cigar box. He fished
out a two-dollar stogie, nipped the end, stuck it between his
ruined lips, and lit it with the match struck on Drake's
desk.

He sat in the upholstered armchair with an arrogant
sigh.

Drake lounged in his chair, watching the disheveled
marshal with an expression of contained fury. He too had
been dished a fetid platter, and he was in no mood to deal
with a troublesome insubordinate.

"Have a drink on me, Nick," he said caustically. "Have
a cigar."

Corey hadn't made eye contact yet, but he made it now.
"So how'd he slip away?"

Drake lifted his arms from the chair, shrugging. His
voice was tense. "I don't know. All I know is he tried wiring
the county sheriff and territorial marshal for help."

"Tried?"

Drake smiled bitterly. "Lloyd Felton from the Western
Union office paid me a visit just after Stillman left. Lloyd
managed to unplug the key from the wire when Stillman
wasn't looking." He took a nervous puff off his stogie. "It
was a close call, though. I don't know what could have
gone wrong. Crawford told me he had some of the best
gunmen north of the Bighorns on his payroll. They
certainly botched this one."

Drake shook his head, and his nervousness over the
situation was told by his haunted eyes. Things had become
worse than he could have imagined. Stillman was not only

alive, but he'd learned of the Gypsy murders and was about to blow the whole thing open. He was back in town, trying to summon help. Now he'd have to be killed for sure, and as soon as possible.

"I take it you ran into him," Drake said, eyeing Corey with disgust.

Corey only shrugged. "The son of a buck took me by surprise. I guess famous lawmen aren't required to fight fair."

"He's still on the prowl I take it?"

Nick puffed the stogie, then removed it to study the coal. "Yeah, but not for long. I'll take care of him, but it's gonna cost you more than what you're payin' me now. You see, I'm tired of doin' all your dirty work and playin' the whippin' boy for the mucky-mucks and gettin' paid peanuts."

"Oh, really! How much is it going to cost me?"

"A bigger piece of the pie."

Drake's fleshy face burned, his jowls quivering, but he managed a haughty smile. "You're even crazier than I thought you were."

Corey leaned forward, his anger making him feel weak and out of control. The unconsidered words came out like steam from a boiling pot. "I wanna cut of the profits, or I'm gonna spread the news around that you ordered me to kill Boomhauer!"

Drake stared at him mutely, getting a leash on his own animosity. "You want a cut of the profits." It was not a question. "You want to play with the big boys, eh, Nick? You want the respect and admiration your badge and gun haven't won you—is that so?"

Corey stared back, unblinking, a sneer drawing his purple mouth back. He didn't say anything.

Drake continued. "The problem, you see, Nick, is that

what you are is all you'll ever be. You're a simple, thirty-a-month-and-found cow waddie. Crawford and I lifted you above yourself when we got you the deputy's job, but you are and forever will be a saddle tramp. The tragedy is that, while you're more devious than intelligent, you aspire to more, and you aspire without the ability to attain. Or at least to attain and to hold."

Corey poked the cigar in his mouth and waggled it with his tongue. "That right?"

"That's right." Drake's voice was level; his eyes prowling behind his glasses like blue oysters. He showed his teeth when he lowered his chin and said, "Now get out of here. Get out of town. And don't ever come back."

The muscles in Corey's face slackened. The last thing in the world he'd expected was for Drake to call his bluff. He quickly removed the cigar. "Huh?"

"You heard me. I've sent a rider for Drake's gun hounds. They'll take care of Stillman. Since they botched the job once, they won't dare botch it again. So, you see, Nick—I don't need you. Big men who know how to handle guns—but who don't aspire beyond their abilities—are a dime a dozen." Drake slapped his hand on his desk; it was a thunderous crack, making Corey jump. "*Good day!*"

Corey stared at him for a long time. Slowly shaking his head, he dropped his cigar on the floor and reached for his gun. "Why, you..."

"It's not there, Nick," Drake said smugly, lifting his own pocket pistol above the desktop and extending it across the blotter. The barrel was pointed at Corey's badge. "But I have one here. If you're not out of my office in ten seconds, I'll use it."

His hand on his empty holster, Nick stared at Drake's revolver. Then he looked at Drake. His lips moved as if he were speaking to himself. He clamped his jaws together and bunched his lips as his anger boiled once more, and he breathed heavily through his nose. A sheen of tears formed over his eyes as he stood stiffly, fists clenched, and walked to the door.

He went out, leaving the door wide behind him. Drake stared after him, knowing he should have shot him.

Chapter Seventeen

AFTER THE FIGHT, STILLMAN WALKED ACROSS THE
creek to the Maclean House. A high-sided wagon loaded
with firewood stood outside the picket fence, and old man
Maclean and a heavy-set Chinaman in logging boots stood
beside it, dickering over the cost of the wood.

Finally, Maclean threw up his hands, growling, "Stack
it behind the house," and the Chinaman bowed and
turned, grinning, and climbed onto the driver's box.

When the wagon had swung around the house,
Maclean turned to Stillman coming up the path. The old
man was heated and scowling. He jerked a thumb to indi-
cate the Chinaman. "He wants twelve dollars a load, and
it's all pine!" Maclean shook his head.

Then he saw the fresh bruises on Stillman's face.

"Ran into your local peace officer," Stillman explained,
his voice still edged with wrath at not only Drake and
Corey but at the whole damn, apathetic town. "He was
trying to savage your granddaughter behind the
mercantile."

The old man's eyes widened for a moment, then

narrowed and turned dark. "So that's why she came running home like the sky was falling."

The furry brows slid down over his eyes, and his withered jaws worked as an expression of fear and helplessness closed over his tired, old face. "That ain't the first time he tried to savage one o' the girls around here. Why, just the other day, he—" The old man stopped and shook his head. He regarded Stillman beseechingly. "What are we gonna do?"

A little surprised by the old man's helplessness after his earlier hostility, Stillman found himself warming to the man. "We're gonna bring him down," he assured him. "I have help on the way."

Skeptical, the old man drew his head back, canting it to one side and squinting one eye.

"I've sent out wires," Stillman assured him. Then, remembering he'd instructed the telegrapher to send the replies he was waiting for to the Maclean House, he frowned and asked, "Haven't I received any messages from the Western Union office yet?"

Gravely, knowingly, the old man shook his head.

Stillman pondered this for a moment. There couldn't be any trouble with the wires. Hell, he'd watched the telegrapher tap the key... "Well, they should be along soon," he said, turning back to the old man. "Just in case anything should happen to me before the sheriff arrives from Chinook, I want you to witness an affidavit and store it in your lockbox. Will you do that?"

"Witness a what?" the old man asked, his skepticism growing. "What the hell's a—"

"It's a sworn statement in writing. I'm gonna tell all I know about what's happened here, naming those I believe to be involved. In the event of my death or disappearance, I want you to give it to the sheriff."

The old man looked dubious.

Stillman put his hand on his arm. "You want your granddaughter to remain afraid of walking the streets in broad daylight, in danger of the man sworn to protect her? You want a cold-blooded killer operating your bank and holding notes on the entire county and working in cahoots with the biggest rancher in the area—a rancher, I'll add, who has seasoned gunmen on his roll?"

The old man looked pale as he studied Stillman, blinking.

Finally, he turned, and Stillman followed him inside, where old Maclean silently gathered paper, pen, and an ink bottle. In the vacant dining room, he sat sullenly across from Stillman while the sheriff, his hat cast aside, scratched his statement on the paper, smoking a cigarette and dipping his pen in the bottle.

When Stillman was done, he blew on the ink and slid it across the table to the old man, who hunkered over it and read it, slowly moving his lips and adjusting his reading glasses. When he was done, he shook his head sadly, sighed regretfully, glanced at Stillman, and picked up the pen.

He scratched his signature in the witness blank and turned to Stillman expectantly. The sheriff folded the document, slipped it into an envelope, sealed the envelope, and gave it to Maclean.

"It's all yours now, Mr. Maclean. Please lock it away. No one else must know of its existence unless something happens to me."

The old man nodded, stood, and walked away.

Stillman had given up hard liquor several years ago, but he now badly wanted a beer to take the edge off his fatigue. It had been a busy couple of days, and the fight with Corey, only a few days after his bout with the Snake-track men, had sapped him. Fortunately, he hadn't taken a direct hit to the ribs, but his muscles were sore, and his fists ached where he'd slammed them against Corey's face.

His general malaise and aching hands added up to the fact he never liked to look at straight on: He wasn't as young as he used to be. But the pick-me-up he wished for would have to wait. While he doubted word of his survival had yet filtered back to Crawford, Drake would know, and at the saloons, Stillman might run into more trouble than he'd bargained for.

Deciding to dally the hour before supper on the porch, pondering his predicament, he headed that way. In a wicker chair between two dining room windows, he rolled a smoke and crossed his boots on the rail.

It was obvious that the rancher, Crawford, had ordered the Gypsies killed. He could have had Boomhauer killed as well, but Stillman didn't think so. Charlie had been shot in the back while excavating the grave, which meant he'd been taken by surprise. Seven riders wouldn't have needed to take him by surprise.

But a single man probably would have waited until his back was turned. And the fact that Charlie had given him his back meant Boomhauer had trusted the man. Which meant the killer was probably his deputy. Corey had probably been ordered by someone other than the rancher, for Crawford, knowing Boomhauer had learned of the Gypsies' murder, would have sent his own men after him.

Drake would have sent Corey.

The big question, however, was why had the Gypsies been killed in the first place? Was it simply because they'd been collaring Crawford's beef? Or was there some other reason?

Why did Stillman keep remembering Drake rushing his daughter to the doctor the other night? The blacksmith had told him she'd gotten pregnant by a boy from the wrong side of the tracks...

A while later, Maclean arrived with an answer to one of Stillman's lesser prayers: a crock jug of honey beer.

"It ain't my best batch ever, but it ain't too bad," the old man said, pouring Stillman a tall glass, the foam piling deliciously. "I keep it in my icebox in the cellar, so it makes a nice cool drink for hot afternoons." Maclean looked furtively through the window, then whispered behind his hand. "My wife, she's a God-fearin' woman and don't approve, so..."

"Mum's the word," Stillman said, taking a tentative sip. He frowned with appraisal and smacked his lips. He smiled. "Not bad, Mr. Maclean." He took another, longer drink. "Not bad at all. Much obliged. Just what the doctor ordered for these worn-out bones."

"Well, I reckon I'm obliged to you, Sheriff. Ever since Drake and Crawford brought Corey to town and talked ole Charlie into makin' him deputy, Lone Pine's been going to hell in a handbasket. Corey worked nights, you see, and while ole Charlie was home sleepin'"—Maclean shook his head balefully—"bad things happened. Stores got broke into, animals started disappearing from people's pastures, and more than one girl... well, more than one girl was assaulted. Most were the painted ones, so they didn't go blowin' around about it, but you could see their bruises just the same. And now that son of a buck—if you'll pardon my language—is going after my granddaughter."

"How is Rachel?"

"She's back in the kitchen, gettin' ready for supper. She said she was all right an' I shouldn't worry, but..."

"I know," Stillman said, wiping the beer foam from his mustache, "you won't stop worrying until Nick Corey is behind bars."

Maclean nodded and rubbed his jaw morosely. "But I don't know what's gonna happen when people find out the banker's in trouble. That's why nobody likes to talk about him—Drake—and his shady business deals and the like. We know if he gets into trouble, we all do. Hell, he and Crawford hold the notes on three-quarters of all the businesses in town. If there's a run on the bank, we'll all go under."

"Not necessarily, Mr. Maclean. The county sheriff will probably talk another banker into covering yours until other investors arrive with enough cash money to make the notes good and keep confidence up."

"Hell, I'm so scared, I'd run down there right now and withdraw everything in my accounts if I wasn't worried everyone else in town would do the same thing."

"That wouldn't be a good idea," Stillman agreed. "Hold on, Mr. Maclean. Lone Pine can weather this storm."

The old man nodded and refilled Stillman's glass.

"Tell me something if you can," Stillman said. "I was told that the banker's daughter got herself in a predicament. You know what kind of predicament I'm talking about?" He'd considered asking the banker but had figured that if Drake wouldn't answer any questions about himself, he sure as hell wouldn't answer any about his daughter.

The old man stifled a grin and nodded sheepishly.

"Do you know by who?" Stillman asked.

Maclean shook his head. "Haven't the foggiest idea. I figured it was some drover since the word is he's of low standing. Much lower than the Drakes would allow." He had to stifle another grin with a snort, brushing his nose with his wrist. "What's that got to do with anything?"

"I don't know," Stillman said, thoughtful.

Maclean turned to go back inside. He stopped and

regarded Stillman cautiously. "So, you think your telegrams got through, do you?"

Stillman had been wondering the same thing, but he shrugged hopefully. "I don't have any reason not to think so."

————

AROUND FIVE-THIRTY, refreshed from the cold beer, Stillman went back up to his room and washed and changed into the extra pair of denims and cotton shirt Nell had laundered for him. His hair slicked down and his mustache combed, he walked back downstairs with the sleeves of the green-plaid shirt rolled up his forearms, his clean, red neckerchief knotted around his neck.

It was only about ten till six, but already the dining room was occupied by five townspeople and a traveling drummer in a gaudy maroon suit. Stillman sat down at a corner table, his back to a wall. Rachel appeared a moment later with the coffeepot and a cup and saucer.

Her hair was swept back in its customary ponytail, and she wore a gray dress he had seen her wear before, but there was something different in her manner. It lay in her slightly tomboyish face, tan from the summer sun, and in her blue eyes—a sadness that was not worry or anxiety, but a kind of generalized despair.

"Coffee?" she asked without expression.

"Please. Are you all right, Rachel?"

She nodded as she poured the coffee. "He tore a good dress, that's all. Are you ready to order or do you wanna sip your coffee first?"

Stillman glanced at the card before him. "I'd like the sirloin and potatoes. Rare."

She nodded. "Sorry I didn't bring the water."

"Huh?"

"The bathwater."

He'd forgotten. "Oh, that's all right."

"I was afraid," she said, keeping her voice low. She glanced at the other tables, then turned back to Stillman. She appeared about to say something else, but decided against it, turned, and walked back into the kitchen.

Stillman leisurely ate his meal and followed it up with two helpings of rhubarb pie buried in whipped cream for dessert. When he'd finished, he headed back up to his room to clean and load his guns. He hoped the fact that he'd sent for help would make him immune to Crawford's gunslicks, but he knew he couldn't count on it.

Whatever the case, he wasn't running. If they wanted to take him down, they'd have to take him down before the town. Let the good citizens of Lone Pine add another murder to their list of secrets.

When he'd cleaned, oiled, and loaded both guns, he read the newspaper he'd picked up downstairs. Around nine o'clock, he went out and sat at the top of the outside stairs. He smoked in the fading light, listening to the sounds of the town hush and die. A freshening breeze wafted down from the surrounding ridges, and coyotes yammered far back in the buttes. A sickle moon climbed.

He'd smoked the cigarette and was crushing it under his boot when the door behind him opened. He stood and swung that way, drawing his Colt. Rachel gave a startled cry and shrank back.

"Sorry," Stillman said with a sigh, depressing the hammer. "You startled me."

She stepped onto the landing, looking cautiously around and drawing the door closed behind her. "Sorry, Mr. Stillman. I guess I'm in the habit of sneaking up on you."

"I'm just a little jittery," Stillman confessed, smiling to calm the obviously troubled girl.

He waited, wondering if she'd only been heading outside—maybe to the privy out back? —Or if she'd been seeking him out. He hoped it was the latter, but he wasn't going to push her. She was a child, after all, and he couldn't expect to get the information from her that he couldn't get from Lone Pine's grown-ups—namely, if and how Drake was connected to the Gypsy and Boomhauer murders.

To his surprise, she asked, "You mind if I sit down?"

"Not at all." He indicated the step he'd vacated.

She sat down, and Stillman stood where he was, two steps below her, one hand on the rail. She obsessively folded her skirts over her knees, and she appeared to be waiting to be prodded.

Stillman obliged her. "Who are you afraid of, Rachel?" Her eyes lifted to Stillman's, though he couldn't see them well in the dying light.

"Whoever killed Sebestyen."

"Who's Sebestyan?"

"The Gypsy boy who was sparking my friend, Sybil."

"The banker's daughter," Stillman said as if answering his own question. Rachel nodded.

A knowing light must have entered Stillman's gaze, for Rachel leaned toward him over her knees and asked, "Is Sebestyen dead?"

"What makes you think he might be dead?" Stillman knew, but he wanted to hear it from her. "Because he hasn't come around in weeks."

Stillman didn't say anything, but Rachel saw the answer in his grim eyes. The girl showed no emotion, but her face paled as she asked, "Was it Mr. Drake? Did he do it?"

"Kill the Gypsy boy? Why would he have done that?"

"Because he didn't approve of Sebestyen, and Seb wouldn't leave Sybil alone. She didn't want him to. She loved him. He kept meeting her in the draw behind their house... and then--"

Rachel's voice fell to a whisper. She looked toward the old barn, one corner of which was burnished by the last of the sinking sun. "And then Syb got in the family way."

There it was, the piece of the puzzle Stillman had been waiting for. Unconsciously, he'd known what it was ever since the blacksmith, Lowdermilk, had told him the banker's daughter had committed the ultimate sin with someone her family did not approve of. He'd just needed someone to say out loud that that someone had been a Gypsy—to hang it out mere in plain sight for Stillman to ponder and scrutinize and connect to the murders.

"You think Mr. Drake did it, don't you, Mr. Stillman?"

Stillman nodded woodenly, thinking it through. "Until just now, I wasn't really sure. I still can't be certain, but I'd bet a fistful of eagles on it."

"What happened to the others?"

Stillman looked at her, distracted. "What's that?"

"What happened to the other Gypsies? They disappeared around the same time Sebestyen did."

Stillman took a long, ragged sigh, and sat down beside her. He placed his hand on hers and said quietly, with deep sympathy, "They're dead, child. All killed by Crawford. Why he killed the whole group, I don't know. I'd guess they tried to fight back when Crawford's gunslicks came gunning for Sebestyen, but who knows? Maybe Crawford wanted them all silenced..."

Realizing he'd been rambling, he stopped and turned to Rachel. She sat with her shoulders hunched, racked with quiet sobs. "All?" she asked between cries. "He killed them *all!"*

Stillman took her in his arms and held her for a long time until her shaking ceased, and her sobs were intermittent. As she moved away from him, he fished a handkerchief from his pocket and gave it to her. She used it to wipe her face and blow her nose.

She said, "Sibyl thought her father had just run Seb out of the county, but I know Mr. Drake better than that. I thought he killed him. I didn't tell Syb that, but..." She let that trail away, and turned to Stillman again, with a pained, bewildered expression on her youthful face. "Why...?"

Stillman shrugged. "Some people are just evil," he said. "There's no explanation for it. There's something in them that good folks don't have. A hate, a kind of meagerness, is how I'd explain it. I don't really know. You see, in some ways, you don't get all that much smarter with experience and age. All I've learned is that wicked men have a strange power that makes them dangerous and cunning and hard to figure."

"Is that why you became a lawman? To stop such men?"

Stillman nodded thoughtfully. "I reckon it is. And to give good folks like you and your granddad and Sybil an edge. Sometimes I succeed, and sometimes I don't."

"Sybil," Rachel said, as though creating the image of her friend before her eyes, on the darkening grass at the bottom of the stairs. "Today, she and I walked down to the draw where she and Seb used to sit together afternoons. We put some wildflowers on a rock. She thinks that by offering gifts to Seb's spirit, she can entice him into coming back to her."

"Sibyl sounds like quite a girl."

Rachel smiled for the first time this evening, but it didn't go very deep. "Some people say she's touched. She just has a good imagination. She reads a lot of poetry and old, old stories—you know, the ones those people from across the seas used to write. I don't set much store by such stories myself—I'm not the reader and thinker Syb is—but I love Syb just the same. She's been my best friend here in Lone Pine, and I needed a friend after my parents died and I came to live with my grandparents. Syb, she doesn't care one bit that I ain't rich like her family."

Stillman let some time pass before asking, "How did she meet Sebestyen?"

"Seb and his father used to cut wood in the draw behind the Drake house and haul it back for Syb's father. The draw was Syb's favorite place to stroll in the summer. She'd sit in the grass and read her books. She saw Seb out there one day and just started talkin' to him."

A miserable chuckle rose up from Rachel's throat. "That's Syb's way. She didn't care that he was a Gypsy. In fact, she thought it was grand that he wasn't like everyone else in Lone Pine. She likes different things and different people."

"Will Drake allow her to raise the baby, or send it off?"

Rachel turned to him with a look of shock and horror. "No! You don't understand," she said. "He—Mr. Drake—had the doctor cut it out of her. He killed it!"

Stillman's heart leaped. Gripped by revulsion, he stared at her blankly, blinking the fog from his brain. "So, the reason Drake rushed her to the doctor the other night. . ."

Rachel's eyes were downcast, fixed on her hands clasped around her knees. "She... she... *bleeds*... and it won't stop sometimes." She squeezed her eyes closed, and tears rolled down her cheeks. "Poor, poor Sybil. She doesn't have the baby, and she still believes Sebestyen is coming back to her..."

Stillman swallowed, scowling off at the weeds at the edge of the yard. "Does Mrs. Drake know about all this?"

Rachel shrugged. "I don't think she knows what Mr. Drake did to Sebestyen, but she knows about the baby." Spite grew in Rachel's voice. "She just stays in her own private bedroom with her door locked, horrified by the scandal of it all, afraid to show her face in the town!"

"Jesus Christ," Stillman groused, lowering his head and running a hand through his hair. He wanted to say more, but he didn't want the girl to hear him curse.

Crawford and Drake would get their due. He'd make certain of that if he had to stay in Lone Pine for another month.

"I best get to bed," Rachel said finally, in a small voice. She rose, and Stillman watched her in silence, having no words with which to comfort her. She opened the door, went inside, closed the door quietly behind her, and was gone.

A half hour later, Stillman was tossing and turning in bed, unable to sleep for thinking of Sibyl Drake and her father and Boomhauer and the Gypsies, when he heard a thump on the outside stairs. Quietly, he slipped out of bed, grabbed the Colt from its holster, and inched the curtain back from the window.

He tensed when he saw two men stealing up the outside stairs, weapons drawn.

Chapter Eighteen

CLAD IN ONLY HIS UNDERWEAR, STILLMAN HEADED FOR the door. He slipped into the dark hall quietly and drew the door softly closed behind him.

In the curtained window of the outside door at the end of the hall, he saw a shadow move. The doorknob jiggled as he padded across the hall and slipped into a linen closet, leaving the door cracked.

The door to the outside stairs opened. Stillman watched two-hatted men in trail garb enter the hall, one before the other. Instantly Stillman could smell the sour stench of alcohol sweat. The second man snickered, and the first man turned to him abruptly, pulling him up by the shirt collar.

"Shut up!" he rasped.

When he was certain the other man had contained himself, the first man turned to Stillman's door. The second man moved up beside him, and both men stood facing the closed door.

They ratcheted back the hammers of their revolvers. The first man whispered, "On three. One, two, three!"

They both lifted their right knees and brought the heels of their boots to bear on the door, smashing it open with

a bang. Instantly, they began firing into the dark room, the explosions of their six-shooters flashing like a raging thunderstorm.

Stillman waited until their hammers clicked benignly against their firing pins, their weapons empty. Then he slowly opened the linen closet door, extending his own revolver and stepping into the hall.

Both shooters were in the room—he could see the vague outlines of their silhouettes through the ghostly haze of the putrid gunsmoke.

Stillman said, "I hope you boys have settled up with your maker, 'cause you're gonna see him soon."

Both men jerked toward him, reaching for second guns. He opened fire, blowing both men back against the wash-stand and dresser, adding his own smoke to that already wafting around his head. The Colt jumped in his hand.

When he'd emptied the gun, he stepped into the room and lit a lamp. He held it high, and the light fell on the two men, one lying on his side before the washstand, the other with his head and shoulders jammed against the wall, chin on his chest. Blood gleamed wetly on them both.

Stillman heard voices in the hall and the sound of hurried footsteps. "What in the name of God!" old man Maclean fairly yelled as he swung into the room, a bulls-eye lantern in his hand. His gray hair was tousled from sleep, and he wore a tattered red robe, open to his white undershirt

"I had visitors," Stillman said. "Tried to air me out a little. Fortunately, I heard 'em coming. Sorry about the room."

"Holy baloney!" Maclean exclaimed in awe, sidling

into the room and looking down with disgust at the two
fresh corpses.

The smell of their alcohol stench mixed with the
sulfurous smell of the powder smoke and blood. Maclean's
frown deepened. "Hey, those aren't none of the seven cold-
steel artists Crawford hired a while back. I mean, they
work for Crawford's brand, but not as gunmen. That's
Frank Tobin and Norvel Ames. They're just thirty-and-
found brush-poppers!"

Stillman had to admit they looked more like waddies
than bona fide gunmen. "Probably in town at one of the
saloons, having a good time, when they heard I was still in
commission. After a few drinks, they decided to try making
names for themselves with Crawford, maybe see if they
couldn't dip into some of that gun money."

"What happened, Mr. Maclean?" It was one of the
other boarders, calling from down the hall.

The old man turned to him. "Billy, go get the undertaker, will you, so we can get these two hard cases out of
here?"

"Right away, Mr. Maclean."

"That's Billy," Maclean told Stillman. "He works
around here for room and board." He glanced at the
bodies again and shook his head. "Well, you gotta know,
Stillman—there's more where those two came from. A lot
more. And a lot more dangerous ones than these two
waddies."

Stillman nodded reluctantly. "I just hope my help
arrives before they do."

"Me too, but it ain't likely. I don't think your telegrams
got through. I think you best head for the hills if you get
my drift. While ye still can."

Stillman thought about that while he moved into a new
room. When the bodies were hauled out of his old one,

and the house finally got settled back down to a nighttime drowse, Stillman did the same and woke up the next morning feeling relatively refreshed, if edgy. Nothing like having a target on your back to make a man edgy, he thought as he shaved in the mirror over the washstand.

But he wasn't leaving town. He would not, could not, run from Crawford and Drake—no matter how many gunmen they had on their roles. He wouldn't give them the satisfaction. He was the only real law left around here, and he would not make a joke of justice by putting his tail between his legs—even if it was the smartest thing to do.

When he'd downed a hurried breakfast, he started out for the Western Union office, keeping a wary eye on his backtrail. Nothing seemed out of the ordinary, however. Children ambled to school with their lunch buckets, and businessmen washed their windows and swept their walks. Farm wagons rolled into town loaded with cream and eggs and buttermilk. No gunmen appeared to be positioned on rooftops or in the gaps between buildings, waiting for a shot at him.

That could mean one of two things, he judged. Either his wires had gotten through, and Drake and Crawford were afraid to make a move on him out of fear of increasing the trouble they were in, or his wires had *not* gotten through, like Maclean suspected, and Drake and Crawford were complacently biding their time.

He hoped like hell it was the former, but when he walked into the Western Union office and saw the guilty, nervous look on the face of the telegrapher, he had a feeling it was the latter.

Leaning against the doorframe, Stillman crossed his arms on his chest and said, "Now, don't you look like the dog fox in the pullet house."

"What... what do you mean?" the stout telegrapher

asked, rising from his desk and moving to the window. His face and ears were flushed, with patches here and there of porcelain white. His smile was manufactured.

Stillman tossed his notes onto the counter and shoved them under the cage grate. "I'd like you to send those one more time."

He reached under the grating and inspected the key, making sure it was hooked up to the wire. "And this time, if they don't go, you better hope your wife has your burial suit all washed and ready for business."

Backing up the threat, Stillman unholstered his Colt, thumbed back the hammer, and aimed it through the cage. Only when the nervous, perspiring telegrapher had ceased tapping the key, and an acknowledgment had been tapped back through the line, did Stillman depress the hammer and reholster the gun.

"Much obliged," he said ironically, tipping his hat to the man, turning, and heading back east on Crawford Street.

He'd just turned toward the hotel when he stopped suddenly, remembering the questions he'd wanted to ask the doctor concerning Boomhauer's body. Mounting the outside stairs along the east side of the mercantile building, he climbed to the door at the top, where DR. LOWELL PERCIVAL, M.D., was ornately stenciled on the glass. On the frame beside the door, a weathered card hung from a rusty nail. Hand-printed letters announced, "Will exchange services for cash money or choice beef cuts only!"

Stillman saw a pale face in the window to his right. The face disappeared, jostling curtains, and footsteps sounded within, growing in volume.

Presently, the door was opened by a tall, long-faced man clad in a well-cut business suit. The man's skin owned the sallow, unhealthy pallor of one who rarely ventures out of doors. His coarse, red-blond hair was brushed to one side in a heap.

He primly cleared his throat, and when he spoke, Stillman detected a trace of an English accent. "May I help you?"

"Ben Stillman. Hill County sheriff. May I have a word?"

The man glared at him for a full five seconds before bunching his lips nastily and drawing the door wide. He turned and walked through a small waiting area with three ladder-back chairs and a spittoon, and entered an even smaller office adjacent to an examining room. He sat in the swivel chair behind a small, neat desk, and leaned back on the coasters, making them creak. He shoved his long, waxy fingers into his vest pockets.

A battered cuckoo, the only wall adornment besides the doctor's framed credentials, ticked monotonously. The air reeked of carbolic acid.

"Are you still hanging around?" Percival asked haughtily as Stillman entered the office, his hat in his hands.

Stillman chuffed a laugh. "Never been so welcomed by a town in my life." He sat in the chair before the desk. "Do you realize twelve peaceable Gypsies were murdered near here?"

The doctor's light-brown brows furrowed slightly, a question working his pupils. Stillman doubted he knew about the mass killing—Drake and Crawford would have kept that quiet. He probably had his suspicions, though. Like everyone else in town.

But he said nothing, just sat there with his hands in his pockets, and stared.

"Want to know why?" Stillman asked.

"Not really," Percival replied. "In a town like this—a growing town, a town cut out of the raw frontier—it's best to let nature run its course. I set the bones and sew the wounds and keep my questions to myself."

More angry at the town's apathy than he'd realized, Stillman persisted. "They died because one boy—one innocent boy—fell in love with a girl and impregnated her. You know who I'm talking about because you treated her." Stillman's lip curled distastefully. "If you can call it treatment."

Percival's face flushed with anger. "How dare you come in here and start slinging around your insults! He was a filthy Gypsy, for godsakes! She was an innocent child, with more brains than common sense, and—"

"Is that how you justify it to yourself? Is that how you justify the slaughter of the whole encampment?"

Percival said nothing. His eyes were flat as a coiled diamondback's.

"How 'bout the murder of Charlie Boomhauer?"

"That was those Gypsy rustlers. If they were rustling, by God, they deserved what they got. They were beggars, vagrants, worthless...!"

Stillman laughed caustically, shaking his head. His laughter died abruptly, and his eyes turned cold as he set them on Percival. "And I bet you consider yourself an educated man."

Indignant, Percival bolted forward in his chair and snarled, "What in the hell did you come here for anyway?"

"You must've seen Boomhauer's body. Did you?"

"Yes, Mrs. Boomhauer sent for me, but there was nothing to be done. I—"

"He was shot in the back," Stillman said. "Was it at close range or long?"

Percival sighed tolerantly and pursed his lips. "I'd say it was close range, from the powder burns."

"Did you dig the bullet out?"

"Yes, Mrs. Boomhauer wanted it removed."

"Did you keep it?"

Percival shrugged and looked around. "I believe so. I suppose you want to see it?"

"Please."

Percival scowled and pushed himself out of his chair. "It'll take me a minute."

He moved to a cabinet with many small drawers. He pulled out several drawers before he found what he was looking for. He gave the small, flat-sided ball to Stillman, who took it between thumb and index finger, inspecting it carefully.

"Forty-four Colt," he said, musing. "Looks like a cap-and-ball. You can tell by the grain twist of the rifling."

"So?"

"So who around here carries a cap-and-ball anymore? Nick Corey does. Carries a big Colt Dragoon. No doubt likes how scary it looks and the size of the hole it makes."

"Well, I don't know anything about that," Percival grumbled guiltily, turning away and rubbing his jaw.

Stillman watched him. Then he got up and left the office, walking to the small, sashed window overlooking the outside stairs and the street. Looking out, he asked speculatively, "You have a right nice view of the street here, don't you, Doc? A bird's-eye view of the livery barn and the jailhouse."

Still at his desk, Percival said nothing.

"I bet you could tell me," Stillman continued, "when the deputy left town the day Boomhauer was shot. I bet you could tell me if the deputy followed Boomhauer several hours later, or just a few minutes later. I have a feeling you spend quite a bit of time at this here window when business gets slow."

Stillman looked into the office, where Percival sat

scowling in his chair, flushing. "Even if I could, what difference would it make?" Percival asked.

"You know the difference. The way Corey's story goes, he rode out looking for Boomhauer only after Charlie had been gone several hours. I'm betting he was sent out by Drake only a few minutes later—to kill him before he could dig up the bodies."

Percival's eyes dropped to his blotter. He said nothing, knowing what kind of man Corey was and not wanting to get involved. The doctor was a bona fide coward, and his silence was answer enough.

Pocketing the bullet, Stillman walked out the door. He was about to descend the stairs and head for the livery barn when a cry rose from the street. Stillman shuttled his gaze across Crawford.

There on the corner, clinging weakly to an awning post, was a blond woman in a red dress. But then Stillman saw that the dress was not really red.

It only looked that way because it was covered with blood.

Chapter Nineteen

STILLMAN TURNED TO HIS LEFT, POUNDED ONCE ON Percival's door, yelled, "Doc!" and ran down the steps and across the street. The girl had dropped to her knees and was falling sideways to the ground when Stillman caught her, his hands instantly bloody.

"Help..." the girl tried, in a barely audible voice. "H... elp... m-e..." Then her muscles relaxed, her eyes closed, and her head fell to the side.

"Miss," Stillman said, easing her to the ground. He turned his head to see Percival, now wearing a black jacket over his vest and carrying a medical kit, walking toward Stillman on his long, thin legs.

Stillman turned back to the woman. He guessed she was in her mid-to-late twenties. Her blood-splattered face was already pale, and the arm in Stillman's grasp was growing cold. Through the blood-soaked dress, he could see the deep slashes across her chest and belly. Another ran diagonally from her jaw to her cleavage. The cuts had been made by a wide-bladed knife or a cleaver—by someone in a fit of manic passion.

"Dear God!" Percival said, standing over Stillman and the girl. He squatted down, wincing at the grisly scene, and touched a finger to the woman's neck. "She's gone." The doctor looked around warily. "Who in the hell did this to her?"

Stillman was looking around too. The man who owned the shop across the boardwalk had come out, and he stood stiffly before his window, looking ashen, his eyes on the woman. A young hostler was moving curiously toward the scene from the livery barn across the side street.

"Anyone see who cut this woman?" Stillman asked, standing and glancing at the shopkeeper, then swinging his questioning gaze to the stable boy. Stillman held up his hand. "Hold it there, son. Don't come any closer."

"I didn't see nothin'," the boy said. Turning to his right and gesturing north on Montana Avenue, he said, "Flo— she comes from thataway."

"Flo?" Stillman asked to no one in particular.

"Flo Kavanaugh," Percival said. "Corey's woman's sister."

"Corey," Stillman said softly, feeling the hair under his collar tighten. What in the hell was the Lone Pine marshal up to? Had he gone completely crazy?

Turning to the doctor, Stillman asked, "Where does he live?"

"Little house behind the jail."

"You better follow me, in case anyone else is injured."

Stillman started across the street. Walking quickly, he headed around the livery barn. He hadn't needed directions to Corey's house, for the wounded girl had blazed a vivid path of blood back to a sun-scorched yard in which clothes hung from a makeshift line, then up the worn footpath to the sagging porch.

Stillman drew his revolver, topped the steps in a single

bound, and pushed through the half-open door. Looking around the cluttered living room, he felt his innards tense, recoiling at all the blood.

The place looked like a slaughterhouse. Even the walls were splattered, as though someone had taken a full bucket and tossed it this way and that.

"Anyone here?" Stillman called.

Receiving no reply, he looked into the kitchen and then treaded through smeared blood into the bedroom. He stopped in the door, his gun extended, wincing. On the bed lay a young brunette woman facedown and nude. She lay with her head toward the foot of the bed, one bloody arm hanging over the edge.

She was so badly carved that there was no doubt she was dead.

His stomach churning at the heavy, metallic odor of the blood, Stillman walked back to the front door, hearing voices. Stepping onto the porch, he saw the doctor talking with a short, heavy-bosomed, gray-haired woman in a black scarf and purple dress and wearing boxy, black shoes. As Stillman descended the steps, the woman threw up her hands, crying something in German, and turned away, ambling out of the yard as she shook her head.

"It was Corey," Percival said, turning to Stillman. "Mrs. Gutner said he left the house about fifteen minutes ago, looking crazy. He had blood on his clothes."

"Which way did he go?"

"North. Anyone inside alive?"

"No," Stillman said. "Get the undertaker. I'm going after your peace officer."

Stillman walked around the clothesline, picking up blood smears in the short, dun grass. He followed the smears through several yards and a small hog pasture before making the road heading north out of Lone Pine. The boot prints continued northward along the road.

Where in the hell was Corey going?

Hand on his gun butt and following the fresh, blood-smeared prints in the dust, he quickened his pace.

———

NICK COREY HAD NOT SET out to butcher the two women he lived with. But when he awakened that morning after only two hours of sleep—he'd stayed up all night drinking and fantasizing about what he could do to finally get some respect around here—something snapped in him.

He felt it before he even got out of bed. And then Biloxi burned his bacon again, and overcooked his eggs and her fat, worthless sister gave him a snooty look as she lit a cheroot. A hot, white heat blazed deep within him and pushed outward into every extremity until he could no longer control it.

That was when he fetched his hunting knife from the kitchen and went to work on the women, whose screams he silenced before either could make it to the door.

Then he strapped on his big pistol, donned his hat and headed outside. He had not realized he was heading to the Drake house until he'd taken the leftward fork branching off the main road and was strolling through the cotton-woods, the big house looming before him, taking the morning light at a pretty angle, touched ever so gently with salmon.

He swung around to the side of the house, mounted the porch, and didn't bother knocking on the kitchen door. He just twisted the knob and walked in, startling the black maid frying bacon on the range.

"Ah, mercy, Mr. Corey! You done frightened my soul!"

"Oh, gosh—I'm sorry about that Henrietta!" Corey exclaimed, moving toward the frilly-aproned woman with long, swift strides, pausing only to remove a fire poker from its stand.

The woman's eyes grew large as she watched him close on her, lifting the black iron poker above his head. He was moving too fast for her to comprehend what was happening, and before she could scream, he'd brought the poker down hard on the top of her skull. As she slumped to the floor, he swung the poker from the side, knocking her against the wall, down which she slid to the floor, where she lay quivering, dying.

"Henrietta, what's all the commotion in there?" Wilfred Drake called from the next room. "And if breakfast is going to be much longer, I'll need more coffee!"

Corey dropped the bloodstained poker and looked around for a leather mitt. Finding one, he grabbed the gurgling percolator off the range.

"Comin' right away, Massa Drake!" he squealed in the exaggerated accent of an African slave, pushing through the swinging door to the dining room.

Drake sat at the end of a rectangular table covered with a white linen cloth and tricked out with two silver candelabras on either side of a vase stuffed with yellow flowers. Drake had heard the peculiar voice and had turned to the door as Corey came through, grinning and carrying the coffeepot.

Drake's face paled, his eyes bright and unblinking as if he could not trust his senses. No, it could not be a blood-splattered Nick Corey walking through that door carrying a coffeepot! Drake had fallen asleep and was only dreaming.

The mock-truckling slave voice came again, high-pitched and vulgar. "Here's yo' coffee naw, Massa Drake, just liken ye orrded. Have de whole damn pot!" Corey slammed the pot on the table. Coffee sloshed up through the spout and stained the cloth.

Gasping with fright, Drake broke out of his shock. He reached for the double-barreled derringer he'd started wearing in his vest pocket. Before he could get his hand on it, Corey drew his big Dragoon, rammed it against Drake's forehead, and clicked back the heavy hammer.

Drake froze. With his free hand, Corey reached into Drake's right vest pocket and withdrew the derringer. He looked at it, smiled, and shoved it into the left breast pocket of his own shirt.

"Nasty little things, derringers," he said thoughtfully. "They can leave a hell of a hole for their size." He pressed the barrel of his revolver harder against Drake's head. "Nothing like what a Colt Dragoon can do, though. You know what I mean?"

Drake's head was forced back in his chair, chin up slightly. His face was skull-white, and his lips were drawn painfully back from his lips.

"Please... don't... what... do you want?"

Corey left the gun there, listening to Drake pant and groan and sigh, silently pleading for his life, squeezing his eyes closed as he waited for the bullet. Finally, Nick withdrew the gun, leaving a small, round indentation in Drake's forehead, and depressed the hammer.

"What do I want?" Corey asked casually. "What do I want?" He turned and walked around thoughtfully, a finger on his lower lip. "All I want, Mr. Drake, is breakfast. How does that sound? A good, home-cooked breakfast for a change, instead of those damn cafe breakfasts I always have on account o' my girl can't cook water without burnin' it."

He turned to the stricken Drake and grinned his Corey grin. "That's all." The grin died completely. "Then I'm gonna kill you and burn your house down. How does that sound, Mr. Drake?"

Drake started out of his chair, bolting, but Corey caught him and threw him back down. Then he grabbed Drake's cloth napkin and used it to tie Drake's hands behind his chair.

"What do you want?" Drake asked. "I'll give you money, silver. Hell, I'll even give you what gold I have... if you'll leave."

"Yeah, you'll give me money, all right, but after breakfast, when I've had my fill. And then I'll take your money and kill you and your family and burn your house down."

"Oh, God!"

"Shut up, or I'll—'"

Corey stopped when a woman's outraged voice sounded behind him. "What is the meaning of this!"

He turned to see the black-haired Mrs. Drake standing in the doorway between the living and dining room, in a long satin wrapper. Her face was deep-lined and wan, as though she'd been asleep for years, and her netted hair was in tufts.

Corey smiled with mock warmth. "Well, if it ain't just the person I've been wanting to see!"

Mrs. Drake stomped her slippered foot *"Wilfred, what is the meaning of this!"*

"Oh, don't blame him," Corey drawled. "It's my fault. I stormed in here and killed your maid and tied up your husband, and shortly I'm going to murder the whole Drake family—father, mother, and little Miss Booksmart. After that, I'm going to steal all your money, burn your house down, and drift on out of town to make my mark elsewhere."

The woman stared angrily, nostrils swelling and contracting. "But right now, I'm hungry," he went on. "Go make me an omelet. Ham and onion. Salt and pepper it good. I don't like 'em runny, but not dry neither. I'll have it with potatoes and toast and a hell of a lot of jam. Steak on the side. I prefer apricot jam, but I'll take whatever you got."

Mrs. Drake stared wide-eyed and tongue-tied at her husband.

"Get in there!" Corey shouted, grabbing her arm and thrusting her toward the kitchen.

He threw her so hard she cried out, nearly falling, and slammed the wall beside the swinging doors. She turned her exasperated eyes on Corey. "I don't... I don't *cook!"*

Corey grabbed the woman's arm and shoved her into the kitchen, following her in. "You do now, Ma unless you want something very painful to happen to you." He gave her another shove toward the range, where the bacon the maid had started had cooked down to tiny, black slivers floating in foamy, yellow grease.

When Mrs. Drake saw the dead maid, she let out an animal squeal. Corey ignored it as he shoved a heavy baking cabinet in front of the outside door, so the woman couldn't escape. Heading for the door to the dining room, he regarded Mrs. Drake with annoyance. She was facing the dead maid with hands clawing at her face.

"Get to it, you homely girl," Corey said. "I'm hungry."

Then he went into the dining room.

"Well, then," he said with a weary sigh, grabbing Drake's coffee cup, tossing the grounds onto the carpeted floor, and filling the cup from the pot. Lifting the cup to his lips, he shook his head. "Busy morning."

He drank and was putting the cup back down when he heard a door open and close. Soft footsteps sounded,

drawing near. Corey swung toward the living room, dropping his cup and clawing his big revolver from its holster,
thumbing the hammer back.

When a slight, brown-haired girl in a light wool poncho
appeared in the doorway to the entrance hall, she gasped,
slapping a handful of fresh-picked flowers to her chest.

"Oh!" she said, breathless, her smooth cheeks pale.
"What's... going on, Father?"

"Why in the hell you asking him?" Corey asked,
annoyed. "I'm the one holdin' the gun."

Behind him, Drake moaned miserably.

The girl's brown eyes had a sensitive, intelligent light.
They frowned as she sized up the situation. "You're Mr.
Corey," she said wonderingly, dropping her eyes to his gun,
then sliding her gaze to her father, who sat at the other end
of the table, at once outraged and dejected, his arms
pinned behind his back, shoulders bulging forward.

"Yes, ma'am, I'm Nick Corey," the marshal said, his
gleaming eyes sliding up and down the slight girl's subtly
curved frame. Slowly, he moved toward her. "And you
must be Miss Sybil."

Her cautious eyes on Corey, the girl said nothing. She
stood frozen in the doorway to the entrance hall, still
clutching the bouquet of fresh-picked wildflowers to her
chest.

"I've heard a lot about you, Miss Sybil. You're the little
girl that caused all the ruckus in town." Corey sidled up to
her, grinning, his eyes taking her in greedily, the musky
scent of her perfume kindling an old hunger.

He lifted his right hand and gently brushed the curly
hair back from her cheek, still flushed from her morning
stroll. "You're the one who was givin' it for free to that
Gypsy"—he leaned close, sniffing her hair—"till your old
man had him killed."

As if awakened from a dream, the girl tensed and whipped her head toward her father. "What?" she whispered.

Drake dropped his eyes to the table. Mrs. Drake was knocking pans around in the kitchen.

"Didn't you know that, my sweet?" Corey asked the girl. "Sure, your daddy had the Gypsy rat shot. Him and all the rest of his Gypsy rat clan."

The girl's soul appeared to take flight, leaving her standing staring expressionlessly at Drake, a husk of her former self. Her brows furrowed, smoothed, furrowed again.

"I thought... I thought you only sent him away," she said to her father, breathless.

She stood there as though catatonic, staring sightlessly at her father, apparently oblivious to Corey nuzzling her neck. Suddenly, he grabbed her poncho and dress with both hands and ripped them savagely, tearing them off her slender shoulders and peeling the dress down to her waist, exposing her small, firm breasts, the color of porcelain. Hooting like a child at a circus, Corey bent low and licked each breast in turn.

Then, when her mind had taken in the information, Corey had given her and had drawn the inevitable conclusion—that her father was indeed capable of such a deed, and that it was the only explanation for the disappearance of all the Gypsies including Sebestyen—her eyes rolled back in her head. Her knees gave, and she slumped toward the rug.

Catching her with an arm around her waist, Corey said, "Oh, no, you don't! Not before I've had me a taste of what you were givin' that Gypsy rat!" He shook her viciously. "I ain't screwin' no dead fish, ye hear!"

He started dragging her through the dining room

toward the living room. Halfway there, she slipped from his grasp to the floor, where she lay inert on her side.

"Oh, no, you don't!" Corey raged.

"Please..." Drake begged. "Please, Nick... don't do this!"

"Wake up!" Corey yelled, kicking the girl's side with his boot. "Wake up, damn you." His face was red, his teeth bared, his muscles tensed. He aimed his big gun at her. "Damn you, wake up, or I'll...!" He thumbed back the trigger, aimed the barrel at her head. "I'll—"

"Hold it, Nick."

Corey turned to the familiar voice, saw Stillman standing in the doorway to the entrance hall, his Colt revolver extended, aimed at Corey's head. Stillman was sighting down the barrel with one eye squinted under the brim of his big, cream Stetson.

As he glowered at Stillman, Corey's face turned pale. Then it colored up some, and he laughed. "What are you doin', Stillman? You come to avenge the great Charlie Boomhauer's murder? He weren't nothin' but a broke-down cowboy. He needed to go. It was time."

Stillman glanced quickly at Drake, then back to Corey, reading the insanity in the young man's eyes. Knowing his charade as a lawman was over, he'd snapped, and he was getting even with any and all who'd slighted him.

"He was twice the man you are, Corey. Ever could have been. So you did kill him."

"Sure I killed him." Corey gestured at Drake with his gun. His voice was dead calm, like the air before a storm. "On his orders. But I was gonna kill the son of a buck anyway. That stupid old cowpuncher was in the way around here. He was in my way. So I killed him, just like I'm gonna kill Drake's princess—right here, so's he can watch and remember me by it."

Corey swung his gun down, aiming at the head of the

girl, who was now conscious and sobbing, curled in a fetal position on the floor.

But before he could fire, Stillman triggered his .44. The report filled the room, pungent smoke wafting. The slug took Corey through his neck. He rocked back on his heels, staggering and grunting, arms falling to his sides. He dropped the Dragoon.

Grabbing the oozing hole in his neck, he twisted around, staggered into the living room, turned again, and stumbled against a table, knocking off two framed photographs and two red candles as he sank to his butt at its foot.

His face was startled, vaguely bemused. Blood pumped from his wound. He tipped his head down and sideways, trying to look at the hole in his neck, then lifted his eyes to Stillman with a confounded smile.

"Damn you," he said weakly. "Damn you to hell. Never... let a guy... have any fun..." Then his eyes rolled back, and he pitched to the carpet, dead.

Chapter Twenty

STILLMAN TURNED TO THE GIRL, WHO LAY whimpering on the floor. He dropped to his knees, gathered her in his arms, rose, and carried her to a fainting couch in the living room, beside the piano and under the head of an enormous bison bull.

Leaving her there, crying and shaking her head as though at something she couldn't possibly believe, Stillman turned to the dining room. Drake sat at the table, his face drawn and expressionless.

"My wife," he said. "She's in the kitchen."

Stillman followed Drake's glance to the swinging doors, pushed through, and stopped. The woman sat on the floor, her back to the wall, gazing up at him wretchedly.

"Who are you?" she asked in a trembling voice.

"Sheriff Ben Stillman. It's all right. You best see to your daughter."

He helped the woman to her feet, and as she moved past him through the doors, he saw the maid lying by the range.

"Jesus God."

He moved to check her pulse but stopped when he saw the blood in her hair, the lifeless eyes staring sightlessly through half-closed lids. Turning, he went back into the dining room.

Drake watched him; his hands still tied behind his back. He didn't appear in any hurry to have them freed.

Seeing the defeat in the man's eyes, Stillman freed him. "Even if you wanted to run," Stillman told him, "you wouldn't get far. I've got help on the way."

Drake shook his head as he rubbed his wrists. "I know, but they won't get here in time to save you. I sent for Crawford's riders last night. They probably rode in this morning, looking for you now."

Drake's eyes grew distant as he listened to his wife cooing to his sobbing daughter in the next room.

His eyes returned to Stillman standing before him. "If you'd give me your gun, I'll just step outside for a moment..."

Stillman shook his head. "I'm not gonna be a party to your suicide. You put yourself in a lonely, god-awful place, and I'm not going to help you out of it."

Stillman turned and went out. He was walking down the sun-mottled lane toward the main road when a gun cracked behind the house. He didn't slow his pace until he'd reached the outskirts of town.

Stopping, he looked around. An eerie quiet had descended, and there was very little movement on Crawford Street ahead. The back of his neck warmed, and his chest constricted.

"Stillman."

He turned left. The blacksmith stood in the yard of his shop, holding a sledge. The puppy sat behind him, a curious cant to its head. Lowdermilk said softly and without expression, "They're here. Just up the street. They're lookin' for you."

Stillman looked toward Crawford Street, where nothing moved, morning sunlight bathing the intersection. His mouth went dry, and his heart picked up its rhythm.

"Thanks," he said, drawing his revolver.

He jogged up toward the intersection of Crawford and Montana Avenue, sidling up to the building on the right-hand corner. Removing his hat, he edged a look around the barbershop, looking east down Crawford.

The street was quiet, with only several horses—saddle horses shiny with trail dust and lather—tied to hitching posts on both sides of the street. There were no buggies or wagons anywhere, and the boardwalks looked like those of a ghost town, shingles creaking in the wind.

Then Stillman heard voices and saw two men appear from a space between buildings, mount the boardwalk, and begin tramping in his direction, spurs chinging on the planks. He jerked his gaze back behind the barbershop, but not before he'd seen the Winchesters the men were carrying at the ready. They wore big hats, prominent revolvers in low-slung, tied-down holsters, and cartridge belts, the brassy shells gleaming in the sunlight.

In their muffled conversation, Stillman heard them mention the livery barn. Turning, he ran back down Montana Avenue, then crossed and entered the livery from the rear.

Outside, the men approached the livery's front door.

"I'll open the door," one said to the other. "Then we'll move in quick, out of the light. Ready?"

Nibbling his handlebar mustache and squeezing his Winchester in his gloved hands, the second man nodded.

The first man lifted the plank bar and heaved on the right-side door, swinging it outward. Before it had sailed wide, the two men dashed into the barn, stepping into the shadows on opposite sides of the doors.

They stood listening.

Finally, they walked side-by-side down the aisle, between the rows of stalled saddle horses who shifted and craned their necks to watch the intruders, swishing their tails suspiciously.

The men were a quarter of the way down the aisle when something sounded in the shadows before them. They stopped abruptly, bringing up their rifles. Looking toward the other end of the barn, they saw the trough-shaped manure bucket attached to chains and coasters on a ceiling track shoot toward them, picking up speed as it came, thundering.

Both men fired, their bullets sparking off the steel bucket. Neither man had time to jack another shell in their rifles before the bucket plowed into them, catching them shoulder high and smacking them viciously. Cursing, they hit the floor hard on their backs, dropping their rifles.

Smashed faces bleeding, they scrambled to their feet and reached for their rifles, turning toward the bucket, which had stopped abruptly behind them, at the end of its track. Before they could bring their rifles to bear, Stillman jumped out of the bucket, crouched, and raised his Colt.

It roared twice, flashing and smoking. The gunmen screamed as they tumbled onto the straw-strewn floor and lay shuddering.

His Colt still smoking, Stillman wheeled and poked a look out the open front doors. West on Crawford Street, two men were running toward the livery, rifles in both hands, dusters blowing out behind them.

Stillman bolted out of the barn and into the street heading for the other side.

"There!" one of the gunmen running toward him yelled.

Stillman made the other side of the street and continued past the mercantile. He swung around the rear of the mercantile and bolted westward down the alley, crossing Montana Avenue just as the two gunmen did the same, on Crawford Street.

They saw him, took a shot at him, but he'd already swung behind the millinery store. He continued running hard, weaving around privies and woodpiles and trash. When he came to a tobacco shop, he tried the rear door. It opened. He stepped inside, and waited, keeping the door cracked.

A few seconds later, a bearded man with a rifle and green bandanna appeared. The man saw the door swinging faintly in the breeze. Turning toward it, he lowered the rifle to his waist and fired four quick rounds through the wood.

Inside, Stillman hunkered behind a stout tobacco barrel.

The door squeaked open. Stillman jumped up from behind the barrel. The man stood there, his eyes widening in surprise as Stillman fired once, taking the man through the heart, throwing him back into the alley, dead before he hit the trash-littered ground.

Three down. Four to go. And Crawford had to be here somewhere.

Not wanting to be trapped in the tobacco shop, Stillman turned and ran through a door. He ran through the main part of the shop, and continued out the front door and across the street, not pausing to look around, but running hard, his Colt clutched in his right fist

"Damnit—there he is!" he heard someone yell from his right as he wheeled around the tinware shop. At the back of the shop, he paused to fill the three empty chambers of his Colt, then bolted up an outside staircase, taking the steps two at a time.

On the first landing, a window stood to his left. He kicked the glass out of the window and jumped through. He waited there in the shadows of what appeared to be a sparsely furnished bedroom—probably the tinware proprietor's private apartment.

Boots sounded on the stairs, and the heavy breath of a man running.

Stillman waited.

The boots paused on the landing as the man inspected the window.

Stillman waited a second, then turned, crouching and extending his Colt through the window, surprising the man standing there with a .44 slug through his belly. The man gave a cry, backed up to the railing, and fell over the side, landing on the stacked cordwood below.

Three more to go, not counting Crawford. The odds were getting better.

Stillman ran out of the bedroom, found the narrow stairs, descended to the store, and hurried down an aisle choked with tin pots and pans to the front. A small, bearded man stood there in a green apron, absently stroking a fat tabby cat and peeking out the window while hiding behind the door frame.

Seeing Stillman, he said, "They just went around the corner. Crawford Street's clear."

"Obliged," Stillman said, opening the door.

"I sure wish you boys would take this trouble out of town," the bearded man said. 'This kind of thing is hard on business."

"Should be over in a few minutes," Stillman assured the

man dryly, stepping onto the boardwalk, wheeling left and jogging eastward.

———

FIFTEEN MINUTES LATER, one of the gunmen stepped out of the alley between the freight office and the drugstore. He saw a face in the window beside him, jerked his rifle that way, then recognized the druggist, who crouched back under the window, out of sight.

Turning to his right, the gunman watched two other gunmen cross the street, heading toward him.

"Anything?" one of them asked.

"Nothing," the first man said. He turned to the bank. Crawford and his big bodyguard, Curtis Clemens, were standing on the corner of the boardwalk, before the bank's front door. The first gunman lifted his hands and shoulders, shrugging at Crawford.

"Fan out and find him!" Crawford yelled.

Turning to his compatriots, the first man said, "All right, Les, you take the—"

He stopped short when he heard a noise like crates falling in the alley behind him. Frowning, he turned that way. "You boys go around the other side," he whispered.

The other two disappeared around the drugstore. Clutching his rifle out before him, the first man began moving back down the alley. He stopped when he saw someone appear from behind a pile of shipping crates to his left, but before he could level the rifle barrel, a pistol barked. The slug took him in his right breast, knocking him sideways against the drugstore, numbing his right arm and causing him to lose the rifle.

He fell on his butt, heart hammering, the pain searing, and swung his gaze back to the man who'd shot him.

Stillman was climbing the outside stairs of the freight office.

"Shelton—where is he?"

It was one of the other two men, crouched at the end of the alley, swinging their heads around warily, poised to fire.

Shelton had trouble speaking, for his right lung was fast filling with blood. The pain was intense. Wincing, he said finally, "Up... roof... freight office..."

The two men broke for the stairs. They were halfway there when a gun barked from the rooftop, and one of the two gave a howl, clutching his left side and dropping to a knee. As the other man continued to the stairs, the wounded man fired toward the roof. Stillman returned fire, and the wounded man took a second bullet, this one through the throat. He made a tight rasping sound, and fell on his side, clawing at the ground with his hands.

He died as the other man made it to the top of the stairs. Wary, this man inspected the lip of the roof overhanging the landing. Then he climbed the rail and slid a look onto the flat roof.

Nothing.

Believing his quarry must have jumped onto the next building over, the Snaketrack gunman slid his rifle onto the tin-covered planking and hoisted himself up after it He stooped to pick up the rifle. Just as his right hand closed around the stock, a gun cracked behind him, smacking the receiver with an ear-tolling clang. The rifle skittered from the gunman's grasp.

He twisted around toward the facade, reaching for the Remington on his right thigh. And just as his gloved hand closed on the grip, Stillman—who must have somehow been hiding on the other side of the facade, probably on some sort of lip over the street—fired again.

The Snaketrack gunman howled and grabbed his bloody left thigh, stumbling backward and over the side of the building. Instinctively, he reached for the roof with both hands, catching the overhang and hanging on in spite of the pain searing his thigh.

"Ah, crap! Damn... damn it."

Stillman appeared above him. Looking down, Stillman frowned and shook his head. "Damn," he said, bemused. "I know your face, don't I?"

"Hel... help me, damnit it, I'm... I'm gonna fall...!"

"Sure enough," Stillman said. "I got paper on you back in Clantick. You're Weed Cole's kid brother, Bud. We go back a few years, Weed and I. What in the hell you doin' in this neck of the woods, kid?"

Bud Cole cursed. "What the hell you think I'm doin'," he grunted, his gloved fingers slipping on the overhang, inching toward the edge.

"Yeah, that was a stupid question," Stillman agreed, hunkering down on his haunches and poking his hat brim back off his forehead. "You're iron-ridin' for ole Crawford."

"I'm slippin'!"

"Well, here, let me help you. I wouldn't want you to fall and cheat the hangman." Stillman holstered his revolver and grabbed the gunman's wrist, then set his boot heel hard against the roofing and pulled against it, hoisting Cole onto the overhang.

He removed the revolver from the gunman's holster and tossed it over the roof. Then he threw the man's rifle over as well.

"I reckon you'll keep till I finish with your boss," Stillman said, turning away.

"I need a doctor, damnit!" Bud Cole wailed, clutching his bloody thigh.

But Stillman had already dropped over the roof to the stairs, his boots thumping the planks and pounding up the alley toward Crawford Street.

————

STILLMAN STEPPED onto the boardwalk and cast his gaze at the bank.

Crawford was there, standing on the corner before the front door. When he saw Stillman, he fidgeted, letting his right hand stray to the gun on his hip.

He was a leggy man in a black, bull-hide vest, a narrow-brimmed, black Stetson pulled low over his eyes, and a cream bandanna knotted around his neck. He looked along both sides of the street named after himself, and seeing no sign of his seven gunslicks, set his jaw grimly.

Stillman walked toward him. As he did so, Crawford stepped into the street, directly in front of the bank and the rosewood bay tethered at the rail. He took a challenging stance with his feet spread a little more than shoulder width apart, hands hanging bunched at his sides.

"I guess it's just you and me, eh, Sheriff?"

"I reckon that's right, Crawford."

"You made short work of my men."

"Someone should've taught 'em patience. They'd have me boxed up right now—like they almost had me in that cave."

"I mink you're just better than I thought you were, Stillman."

"You're about to find that out, Crawford."

Crawford's lips stretched a smile under his gray mustache. "Well, we'd best get a move on. Your help's likely to be arriving any minute. I'm gonna need to get your carcass off the street and hauled out of town."

"Your move."

Crawford grinned again. "Curtis?"

Following Crawford's gaze, Stillman shifted his head enough that he could see a man move out from between two buildings behind him and to his left. Stillman couldn't turn that way without giving his back to Crawford.

Which meant the second man had him dead to rights.

"Now you made a foolish move, Stillman," Crawford said, showing his teeth.

Stillman exhaled. He'd thought he'd about finished this mess, and now he was about to be the one who was finished.

Fay flashed in his mind, and all the blood drained to his stomach, making him ill. He'd come so close. So damn close. But now it was slipping away.

He flexed his right hand. If he was going, by God, he'd take Crawford with him.

"Just give me the word, Boss," the man behind Stillman said.

Grinning, Crawford let several seconds pass. Then, calmly, he said, "All right, Curtis."

A gun boomed, and Stillman jerked his own gun up, but he held his fire. Realizing he hadn't been hit, he turned and saw the big man behind him stagger into the street and fall facedown in the dust, a massive hole in his back.

Out from between the buildings stepped old man Maclean and the blacksmith, Lowdermilk, smoke curling from the double-barreled shotguns in their arms.

Sensing Crawford's draw, Stillman jerked back toward the rancher, drawing his own .44. Crawford's revolver had just come level when Stillman squeezed off his shot, catching Crawford in his right shoulder. Crawford fired, but the slug sailed wide.

Crawford dropped his gun, grabbing his shoulder and cursing. Stillman turned toward the hotelkeeper and the blacksmith, standing there looking satisfied with themselves.

"We both used to hunt with Charlie Boomhauer," Maclean said simply.

"Much obliged," Stillman said.

"We've had enough of their brand of horse manure," Lowdermilk said.

Slowly, Stillman walked toward Crawford, holstering his .44. "You're under arrest," he told the red-faced rancher.

"You don't have any jurisdiction in this county!" the wounded man wailed, beside himself with fury.

"No, I don't," Stillman said, grabbing Crawford's collar and giving him a fierce shove eastward down the street.

He kicked him in the ass, sending him stumbling toward the jail. "Just the same, though, I'm gonna turn the key on you, and I'm going to enjoy every second of it."

Epilogue

ONE WEEK LATER. STILLMAN AND MELVIN Bergquist, the Blaine County Sheriff, walked out of the Lone Pine jailhouse and stood on the narrow stoop, gazing around and picking their teeth with sharpened stove matches. It was nearly nine o'clock in the morning, and business was heating up on Crawford Street.

"I think one of the first orders of business—once we have a new marshal and banker, that is—is to change the name of this street. What do you think, Ben?"

Stillman stood with his hands on the tie rail to which his big bay was tethered. The horse was rigged up and ready to start for home. Shaking his head and stomping, Sweets appeared as eager as Stillman felt about getting back to Clantick.

Stillman waggled the match around in his mouth and smiled. "I think Boomhauer Street has a ring to it. What do you think, Melvin?"

Bergquist nodded. He was a portly, balding man with a waxed mustache. He wore a dark jacket and a string tie, and a Colt Lightning resided in the black, tooled holster he wore high on his right hip. "I'll put that to the town council. I'm sure they'll go for it. Charlie helped get this town on its feet. I'm just sorry it turned on him."

"It was Drake, Crawford, and Corey who turned on him," Stillman said. "Charlie was outnumbered and outflanked."

"Thanks again for what you did here, Ben. I'm sorry you had to do it alone."

"Couldn't be helped. I'm just happy the bank's all right, and you have another marshal on the way."

"Yeah, the feller I have coming is a good man. James Stanley and his wife will fit in well here, and I'm confident Jim'll hire a good deputy. As for the bank, Homer Glidden from the Stockmen's Trust in Chinook is gonna cover all the loans until we can find some new investors. Until we do, Homer'll have one of his own managers keep the doors open at least three days a week. Everything should work out fine. It'll be nice to have Crawford's trial over, so the folks of this town can put the bad memories behind them."

"Lone Pine will be fine," Stillman speculated. "With men like Lowdermilk and Maclean leading the way."

He untethered Sweets and climbed into the leather, settling himself in the saddle. "And I'll be back to testify at Crawford's trial. Wouldn't miss it for the world."

"I'll let you know when the circuit judge sets the court date," the sheriff replied. He extended his hand. "Thanks again, Ben. Remember, whenever you need a favor—anything at all—you let me know."

"I'll do that, Melvin. Take care."

"Say hi to that lovely wife of yours."

"I'll do that too. After *I've* said it," Stillman added with a lusty grin, toeing Sweets into a jog away from the jailhouse, heading west.

He slowed when he saw a wagon heading toward him,

behind two whiskered drovers in trail garb. On the wagon's seat sat Nell and Robbie Tobias. Spying Stillman, Robbie waved. "Hello, Mr. Stillman."

"Hello, there," Stillman said, drawing abreast of the wagon and halting.

"I thought you would have gone back to Clantick by now," Nell said, smiling up from beneath the brim of her felt cowboy hat, looking fresh and pretty beneath her wholesome country tan.

"I stayed another week to help Melvin Bergquist get things in order. There's a heap to do when the town's banker, the region's biggest rancher, and the town marshal are all removed from power."

"I bet there is," Nell said, looking around at the bustling street. "But everything looks all right now. People look so... optimistic. I felt it too, as soon as I hit town." She glanced in the wagon bed, at the crock jugs of buttermilk and the eggs stacked in straw-filled boxes. "It's our day for selling our farm goods at the mercantile."

Stillman smiled. There was an awkward silence. Wagons, buggies, and horseback riders moved around them.

"Well, if you're ever back in the country," Nell said, flushing slightly, "come on out and sit a spell. I usually have a stew on the stove, and the coffee's always hot."

"I'll do that, Nell. And if you're ever in Clantick..." He let it trail off and smiled ruefully, for they both knew that they'd probably never see each other again.

And that it was for the best.

Stillman pinched his hat brim. "Goodbye, Robbie. Goodbye, Nell."

They bade him farewell, and he heeled Sweets westward once again. At the edge of town, he turned and looked back. Nell's wagon sat where she'd originally stopped, and she and Robbie were watching him.

Robbie waved, but Nell did not. She turned, flicked the horse's reins, and started eastward down the street.

Stillman turned in his saddle and headed home.

A Look at: Hell On Wheels (Sheriff Ben Stillman Book 8)

BEN STILLMAN'S WILD RIDE!

When Sheriff Ben Stillman accompanies Judge John Bannon and friends to a wedding in Sulfur, Montana Territory, he aims to have a nice long weekend of rest and respite from law dogging. But Angus Whateley has other plans. The crazy ex-Confederate has just been released from prison, and he's out to avenge the hanging of his cattle-rustling sons--hangings ordered by Bannon.

Backed by a gang of the most violent and vicious members of his family, Whateley strikes when the judge takes the stagecoach back home. Soon, Stillman finds himself fighting a wheel-bound war against clan of zealous killers out for bloody revenge...

FROM THE CURRENT KING OF THE SEXY, HARD-DRIVING SHERIFF BEN STILLMAN SERIES!

AVAILABLE MAY 2019 FROM PETER BRANDVOLD AND WOLFPACK PUBLISHING

About the Author

Peter Brandvold grew up in the great state of North Dakota in the 1960's and '70s, when television westerns were as popular as shows about hoarders and shark tanks are now, and western paperbacks were as popular as *Game of Thrones*.

Brandvold watched every western series on television at the time. He grew up riding horses and herding cows on the farms of his grandfather and many friends who owned livestock.

Brandvold's imagination has always lived and will always live in the West. He is the author of over a hundred lightning-fast action westerns under his own name and his pen name, Frank Leslie.

READ MORE ABOUT PETER BRANDVOLD HERE:
https://wolfpackpublishing.com/peter-brandvold/

Printed in Great Britain
by Amazon

38319094R00128